THE PAINTED LADY

JOSEPH FALANK

Winter Goose
PUBLISHING
where words take flight

Winter Goose Publishing
2701 Del Paso Road, 130-92
Sacramento, CA 95835

www.wintergoosepublishing.com
Contact Information: info@wintergoosepublishing.com

The Painted Lady

COPYRIGHT © 2015 by Joseph Falank

First Edition, August 2015

Cover Art by Joseph Falank
Typesetting by Odyssey Books

ISBN: 978-1-941058-32-9

Published in the United States of America

For my two girls
my wife, Rebecca, and my daughter, Madelyn
All the inspiration I need

"Take it from me, Fate doesn't care most of the time."
—Dianna Wynne Jones, *Castle in the Air*

"Where you go, I shall go; where you die, I shall die,
and there will I be buried."
—Rosamund Hodge, *Cruel Beauty*

Drawing a picture can be a long and arduous process; it is capturing a single frame of a single moment of life, whether the subject is based in reality or resides in the imagination. Before an artist can begin The Work they need to feel inspired. The idea must come organically. The idea must also be, above all the others, the one the artist is able to visualize.

The idea is key.

There was no way to know his wife was going to be murdered; the most horrific twist of irony when considering a discussion that took place on their second date some thirteen years earlier. They had been sharing stories of the worst dates they'd ever been on. The kind of thing two people talk about after too much wine.

He spent much of that night staring across the table at the woman he believed far too beautiful for him. This wasn't Miles selling himself short, thinking she was way beyond his league; it's just that he wasn't a complete idiot to the fact that he was the luckiest guy sitting in Tony's Restaurant (and made sure to pray his silent thanks when she got up to use the bathroom). To further drive this point forward came numerous sly gestures of the congratulatory kind from other patrons sitting nearby—winks and nods, even a big ol' thumbs-up from an older man in a pink polo two tables away, he who also licked his rubbery lips suggestively at the same time. Of these silent manners of congrats directed his way Miles was appreciative; of the old man a bit weirded out. It's always nice to know when other people think you've scored well beyond your means.

This girl was indeed beautiful. Stunning, even. Dressed in simple black and pinstripe slacks over leather boots that itched the curiosity as to how high they traveled up her calf, along with a turquoise wraparound sweater that matched her eyes. Her shoulder length auburn hair had been straightened. This, he learned through a prior conversation, took considerable time and patience and effort to rid the natural kink she maintained fresh out of the shower. The enticing image of her stepping out of the tub that popped in his head resulted in another considerable itch of curiosity.

Such distracting thoughts, however, needed to be shoved out of mind. If she caught him not paying attention because he was too busy picturing what she looked like naked there would be a sharp decline in the possibility of that fantasy becoming a reality. He'd already missed out on something she said about her mother having Lyme disease. Or maybe that her mother was allergic to limes. He couldn't remember.

So instead he lingered on the beauty he could see rather than imagined. Her makeup was simple. No bold raccoon eyes, no rosy enhancement of the cheeks; her lipstick was non-existent, only a sheen layer of Blistex to keep them from chapping. She was nothing like the lineup of painted women dolled up in fishnets in the bar at the front of the restaurant, whose heavy application rivaled rodeo clowns and left behind thick residues of ruby red on their downed glasses of Chardonnay.

Those who also sported purchased tans. In the middle of winter.

Miles would not call Stephanie *hot* by any means. He always regarded that term as derogatory. A woman's hotness factor was determined by the amount of add-ons and touchups; tucks here, there, everything defying gravity and age. Barely-there clothing that barely covered up what really wasn't there underneath it all, beneath the glossy surface. Being *hot* never improved upon a terrible personality. And hot women tended to have more mileage on them than a New York City taxi, along with a comparable amount of work performed under the hood.

This woman, Stephanie, wasn't supplemented, augmented, or boosted. She wasn't fake. No Plain Jane either, she was simply beauty and comfort. From her clothes to her fair skin to the way she carried herself. Humble, casual, and confident without an air of pretentiousness. Everything he had been looking for. Everything that made him feel relaxed, feel grounded, when his anxiety wanted to skyrocket him through the paneled ceiling.

And thank God when it came time to order she gave the waiter actual items off the entrée list. If she had ordered a salad, Miles may have gone back to picturing her naked. At that point who cared if he paid attention?

The topic of their worst dates came up midway through their last refill of Pinot Noir. Both were on their fourth glass.

Miles went first.

"Well, does it count if I got stood up?"

Stephanie flashed a pouty frown full of sympathy. "Oh no, that really happened to you?"

He took a shallow gulp from his glass and shrugged in a manner that said *yeah, oh well, what can you do?*

"Why didn't she show up?"

Miles explained, "I should tell you first that this girl had been divorced for a while. We went out a couple of times and things were going really well. She was an NP over at Wilson. We were going to meet up for coffee on a Sunday afternoon after her shift ended. So I got to the café, an hour passed. I tried texting, I tried calling. Nothing."

"So she never said anything?"

"Oh she did," Miles said. He took another sip of wine. "About four days later. She sent me a text and apologized. She said she just couldn't go through with our date because right as she was leaving work she got really sick. Turned out she was pregnant. With her ex-husband's baby."

The reaction was priceless. Stephanie's eyes doubled in size. Her mouth almost made a perfect O, the awe lowering her jaw like a shocked cartoon character. "No way!"

Full of pride, Miles lifted his glass by the stem and tipped it in his date's direction. "Beat that, if you can." He drained what red was left.

Before Stephanie began the story of her worst date she drained the remainder of the wine in her glass as well, about two fingers full, and said she'd need another refill on hand while telling it, but asked, "How long ago were you stood up?"

Miles got the attention of a waiter. "About three weeks ago."

"Did you meet her on the site?" She was referring to LocalSingles. com, the online dating pool where she and Miles had begun conversing a week ago.

Miles nodded. A waiter arrived at their table with a fresh bottle of Pinot. He went through the process of unwrapping the cork and opening the bottle in front of them. Their glasses were filled three-fourths to the rim. Miles paused until the waiter was gone before resuming their conversation. "With the exception of you, that site's been a bust."

Stephanie smiled. "That's nice of you to say, but I saw all the winks and pokes you got on your profile page. There were a lot of girls interested in you. What if I'm keeping you from one of them, maybe the one you're supposed to be with?"

He waited for the rush of the wine to hit his senses. There was the feeling of slick warmth sliding down his throat. He felt a quiver in his stomach that was begging for food but fueling on red. It took a few seconds before the fog of the alcohol blossomed inside of him. "I don't think it works that way," he said.

After a healthy swallow of her own, Stephanie reapplied a thin layer of Blistex. "You don't, huh?"

"There's always a reason for things," explained Miles. He could see it then on her face, that pretty face tinted by the burst capillaries in her cheeks. By the adorable twitch in her nose something had clicked in Stephanie's mind. She leaned in closer, their conversation turning exclusive. Private. The remainder of those in the restaurant were cut off. It was only the two of them that existed now. Miles felt a distinct rise in the temperature around him. That likely had to do with the fact that when Stephanie leaned toward him the V in her sweater opened slightly, revealing a bit more of her skin and the top of the line that began her cleavage. He fought to keep eye contact.

"So then," she said, "are you implying there's a *reason* you and I are here right now?"

The provocative way she worded the question, the emphasis and soft tone she used made him wonder if she was feeling out their situation. She was being quite forward, and this was likely due to her own skimming under the veil of her own alcoholic haze. He liked her, definitely. A lot. But in his current state—where the lights in the room were just beginning to glow soft and puffy—he didn't want to assume anything. This—their second meeting and first official date—had been going perfectly so far. No need to scare her off.

"I just think there's a reason for everything," he said. He then took up his glass in a private toast. "Even the strangest things happen for a reason."

Stephanie hesitated joining him in the salute. "Are you saying our meeting is strange?"

"Not at all." He went on to clarify. "I'm only saying that . . ." he was staring into her eyes, how they shimmered in the light, how inviting they were, how they held him; the droning of the busy restaurant beyond their table lost to his ears ". . . things we've both been through . . . sometimes when they happen they don't make a whole lot of sense . . . but everything always works out. I found a woman who was later impregnated by her ex-husband. That experience led me to you."

He could see Stephanie stifle a giggle. "That's sweet." She raised her glass to meet his. "You're drunk, but I'll toast to that."

"I'm not drunk," he retorted. "You're just amazingly sober."

There was an audible clink to their glasses coming together. They spent a long moment giggling that the glasses hadn't cracked but refrained from becoming obnoxious about it.

This was when their date took a dark turn.

"I suppose it's my turn to tell you about my worst date."

Now it was Miles leaning forward to listen. His shirt was kept buttoned to the collar; no wiry chest hairs or peeks at his protruding collarbone on display.

Right away he knew something was very wrong about this story, even before she spilled a single word of it. He could tell by the light in her eyes, how it dulled. The lights around the room no longer blurred. The somber look on Stephanie's face was enough to sober him up quick.

"This was also a couple of weeks ago," she said. "This one guy . . .

when we were sending messages back and forth he just . . . seemed too good to be true, you know? He was just super sweet. I had no reason to think otherwise.

"But then, one night, right before we were gonna go out, I got this . . . this strange feeling." She placed the flat of her hand inches beneath the base of her throat. "It was like pins and needles, like when your foot falls asleep and you try to move it. In an instant everything felt wrong, just very wrong."

Miles regarded his wine glass, his fingers lightly on the stem. There wasn't even the slightest temptation to take a drink. He asked, "Did you end up meeting the guy?"

She shook her head. "I couldn't get the thought out of my head that something terrible would happen if I did." A pause. "I cancelled and stayed home. Eventually the feeling went away on its own."

Miles flexed his brow. "So nothing happened?"

Stephanie wasn't deterred by her own story. She needed the refill as she had previously mentioned because it was at this point when she paused that she emptied the glass in a single tip. She then wiped her lips with the napkin. "A couple of nights later I saw on the news that this guy had broken into his ex-girlfriend's apartment. He had a rifle. He shot her. He also shot the guy she was with." Somehow she was able to keep at bay the emotions welling in her face. "It could have been me, Miles. What if we met and I told him it wasn't going to work out?"

Miles had no answer.

"That feeling . . . the one I told you about. I think it was my guardian angel looking out for me."

"You believe in them—guardian angels?" Miles hoped he wasn't sounding skeptic, certainly he wasn't meaning to, not to her, not after hearing that story, even if the kneejerk reaction in his gut was one in the same.

Stephanie didn't seem to notice. Perhaps she didn't care whether he believed or not. Her own faith was enough. "That night, when I got that feeling, it was like . . . affirmation, you know? I could sense it somehow."

She had no more wine to make a toast so she lifted her water glass a few inches off the table instead. "It's like you said: Even the strangest things happen for a reason."

He touched his water glass to hers.

Their waiter arrived shortly after their glasses clinked together for the second time holding a large tray with their dinners. A medium-rare sirloin with a side of mashed for him, a creamy white dish of Chicken Alfredo for her. When asked they both declined refills on their wine. Both opted for more ice water.

Miles held the first cut of his steak just inches from his mouth. "Did you get that weird pins and needles feeling about me?"

She looked up, the string of pasta hanging down vanished, slurped between her pursed lips.

"No," she said. "You're a good guy, Miles."

He huffed, mildly, displayed a half-grin. "If this was Jeopardy that would be filed under the category Things Said By Every Girl I Wanted To Date."

She retorted, "Am I like every girl?"

By the curl of a smile forming on her lips, her eyes rekindling in the overhead lights, he sensed that despite the previous downer of a conversation potentially sidetracking their evening, she was keen to getting their night back on track, them getting back to having a little fun. He matched her playful grin. "No," he said. "Not at all."

Under the table something brushed the inside of his right leg down around the shin. Miles about leapt out of his seat until he realized it was one of her legs slinking around his. She had removed one of her leather boots somehow. The touch was her naked calf against him. In an instant a rash of heat rushed into his face. Again he was staring into her eyes, the rest of the world around them falling away.

It was that moment he thought about the rest of the night—the first real touch of her kept him up for hours lying in his bed. Not their first kiss that would come later when he dropped her off (though it was a very close second to his favorite moment), and not even the far more revealing glimpse of cleavage he got when she bent down to get her purse. Her touch, coupled with the sultry look in her eyes, had managed to burrow a hole deep into the well of his soul and find a home there.

Despite the mileage through life they'd rack up together, and despite how years typically wane on a marriage, her touch and her eyes could always plunge him under a spell. They could rouse him, calm him, soothe him, jolt him, send a current under his skin sprouting goosebumps and waves of pleasurable shivers. She never got old to him.

Which was why her look and her touch would haunt him in some of the darkest days that came after her death.

Before an artist can begin their drawing, they must take into account everything of their surroundings, anything that could influence the creation of The Work.

Their surroundings aren't limited to just the environment, but also of their experiences.

It was the unusual sound of something crossing the floor over his head that woke Miles. On any ordinary day it was his bladder begging to be emptied. That happened a lot, he discovered, for only being forty-two. His future urologist, whoever that lucky—and hopefully small-fingered—individual turned out to be, would have a field day with him in the next couple of years. But that was beside the point. His alarm clock was the only other thing to rouse him so suddenly, if he happened to set it. The night before, though, he didn't. No reason to.

And, he was about to discover, this was going to be no ordinary day.

Despite the sound, and why it was so unusual and unexpected, priorities shifted when his eyes opened to a most unusual feeling. A feeling both intimately familiar and, yet, one so very distant, somewhere long behind him, out of reach. A memory. When his mind cleared the haze of waking and made the connection to the touch against his leg, he gasped for breath and scrambled toward the headboard in fright, drawing his legs in so that his knees pressed up against his chest. The two-inch-thick slab of cherry-stained wood hit with a hollow thud against the inside wall. His hastened breaths slowed when the reality set in. He was awake, and all alone.

The sheets were splayed and twisted over the bed top. The light comforter was nowhere within his limited sight. Squinting through nearsighted eyes reduced the bright, blurry haze of the room but still was of no help in making out the bundled sheets around him. The one comfort was the light. Warm rays of sun pierced through the open blinds hung over the two adjacent bedroom windows. It was probable to believe the comforter lay in a heap on the floor beyond the foot of the bed. Another piece of evidence in the case of another restless night. If he'd taken his prescription he would've slept better.

Miles rubbed his eyes, heart jumping but calming, his mind racing, his recall working over the last few moments to ponder and realize his being startled was all for nothing.

The sounds from the floor above—sounds his own mind had to be manufacturing—had slipped into his troubled sleep to wake him. But his imagination wasn't done prodding. As the fog of weariness began to lift, and the gentle song of morning birds welcomed him, Miles's eyes fluttered open. His glasses were on the bedside table but he didn't need them to see the other side of the bed was empty. He knew. Which was why it rattled him to attempt to straighten his leg only to feel something coiled around the inside of his right calf. This something warm, and smooth, much like Stephanie's leg, how she entwined hers with his under the table that night so long ago in the restaurant. How that touch defined many nights they shared in bed. It was one of their married things; a part of their language. A habit of affection.

But now it was an impossible touch.

Stephanie hadn't been there to share a bed in nine months.

Never before had he experienced such a ghostly feeling. Over the nine months that he'd been a widower, Miles had many dreams of her, of specific moments from early on in their relationship, but not once had those dreams reached beyond the barrier separating his imagination from the world that existed once his eyes were open. He continued clutching the twisted sheets in a death grip, his body slick with cold sweat. His pillow was damp and discolored from the many restless nights. The unused pillow on the opposite side of the bed was crisp white and cool. He sent out mental feelers to sense any remnant of that phantom touch of his wife's warm and smooth calf wrapped around his own, the bottoms of her rough and calloused feet, as a result of her tendency to walk around barefoot whenever possible, against his ankle bone. But he felt nothing. She had passed beyond the most desperate grasps of his memory.

He was fully awake, and left with the certainty that he'd imagined the whole thing.

You're going crazy, you know. It's all piling up.

That's why he was seeing the shrink.

And why he was taking the pills. When he felt like taking them.

Those large red pills that sat to the far left on the middle shelf of the medicine cabinet in the bathroom. After the first sessions with Dr. Andrews—the feeling-each-other-out period—the elderly therapist mentioned his growing concern regarding Miles and his . . . active imagination. Bluntly, that it had been getting the better of him. Though there was initial reluctance on Miles's behalf to buy into such a thing and not think he was being suckered because the doc knew he was wealthy, this was a time he had to stop and wonder. It wasn't just strange glimpses out of the corner of his eye or his dreams plaguing him.

Indeed things were escalating.

Before, he would be in the apartment and notice something—a leak dribbling out of the kitchen faucet, as it had been in one instance—and raise his concerns aloud as if Stephanie were in a nearby room. While that seemed innocent enough and understandable given his mourning, what became jarring was when he'd catch himself waiting for her to answer. The steady silence always the brutal reminder. He would then break down and cry. For her, and for himself. Because he knew it wasn't normal.

This speaking out to her would happen on many more occasions. When he felt really defensive about it he'd wonder what was so abnormal. How many children have imaginary friends that they talk to and no one bats an eye? How many sons and daughters ask questions and hold one-way conversations with deceased parents at the grave when setting down fresh flowers? How many people talk to their *pets*? And *he's* the crazy one for talking to his absent wife?

It was upsetting. Because it never felt like he was losing it, yet the evidence against him was stacking up. Undeniable. Miles reached down, ran his hand over the area of his leg where he had felt his wife against him. It had just felt so real. So goddamn real.

Because you want it to be real, Dr. Andrews would say in his soft and passive, non-judgmental rasp. Miles pictured the old man sitting across the room in his black leather chair—bushy salt and pepper eyebrows wrinkling at Miles's extravagant claim of feeling his dead wife's presence beyond his dreams. Andrews would take it all in like a sponge, one that charged eighty-five bucks an hour. A sponge that once said: *Months ago I chalked it all up to grief. Now . . . it's become something else. Metastasized.*

The official label from Andrews was Acute Stress Disorder. Under the layman description of ASD (also known as what Miles could find on webmd.com): *After experiencing a traumatic event, the fragile mind compromises itself while trying to find balance and adapting into a comfortable return to normalcy.* In this delicate state he was to believe it normal to catch a hint of her reflection in a mirror, or off in his periphery. The brief shape of Stephanie passing by, just out of view, always out of reach. Even though he knew what he was seeing wasn't real, he would always turn his head to try and find her.

Shouldn't you be taking your meds now?

Miles bit down hard on his bottom lip, trying to ignore the voice in his head as much as he could. But it was persistent.

He moved to sit on the edge of the bed, feet on the floor, head in his hands. Miles hated the thought of medicating himself, hated how the pills made him feel—uncaring, indifferent. The Ambien staunched the flow of his dreams.

He also hated to admit that the pills helped. They weren't a permanent solution, but enough for the short term. Downing two of the reds made him pretty numb to everything for a while. Within half an hour he could be stretched out in the red recliner, lost in a mindless, drowsy stupor while being bombarded with gab from Rachael Ray or Dr. Phil. Ambien was also quite effective against that annoying talk show duo of Kathie Lee and Hoda. Under the blanket of his pills Miles didn't have a problem in the world.

Maybe he'd take three of them and snooze through the rest of the morning. Three gave him complete, uninterrupted sleep. There would be no phantom feeling when he would wake. It'd probably take him a minute to remember his own name. The marvel of modern medicine. And endless refills.

There wasn't anything planned for the day but a lunch meeting in the afternoon. Before then nothing sounded better than the opportunity to catchup with a few good hours of listless sleep.

He was just about to stand with the intent of visiting the medicine cabinet in the bathroom when the sound that woke him returned. A path of footsteps crossed the floor above.

Miles reached over on the bedside table for his glasses. They couldn't help him see through the stucco ceiling but there was comfort in having them on. He remained still, listening, drawing each breath long and slow as the walking over his head tracked around and then faded away. All he could hear in the following was the song of the morning birds. Miles remained on the edge of the bed a few moments longer, waiting to see if the footsteps came back. They didn't, but still, he was uneasy.

To his knowledge, no one lived in the upstairs apartment.

This wasn't his imagination getting the better of him. Something was moving around in the empty apartment upstairs. Miles had been up to the second floor unit once, about a month ago. He'd gone up out of curiosity after the previous tenant moved out. The plan was if the second floor space had a better layout, he was going to put in with the landlady for the move. As it turned out, the two units in the house were carbon copies. With the exception of a few cosmetic choices in paint, one apartment looked to have been copy-pasted and stacked atop the other. The size and layout of the rooms, the tiled floors of the kitchen, bathroom, and hallway, placement of the ceiling fans, even the arched passageways, the deep carpeting, all of it the same. Even the proximity of the outlets and light switches were identical. Miles dropped the thought of moving. Too much work for no gain.

The second floor unit had been occupied by to an elderly man named Lou. Lou spent many days sitting out on his front porch overlooking the quiet block and mumbling to himself. On occasion Miles would step out onto the front walk and toss up a hello with a wave. Lou was hardly responsive. A man stricken with Alzheimer's according to his daughter Claire, who visited quite frequently. She came to fix meals, run the washer and dryer out in the breezeway, water the plants, and vacuum—oh Lord, the amount of vacuuming done up there; never would Miles had expected one old man could be so messy. It was eventually decided by Claire and her husband to take in her invalid father. The running back and forth and doing routine household duties in two places had taken its toll. Lou moved out. Since then the place sat vacant. Or so Miles thought.

Probably just people checking it out.

It wasn't uncommon for the landlady's grandson, Jimmy, to be showing the place. It was actually more unbelievable that the apartment had sat empty for the last month. The house was located in a very decent neighborhood that housed mostly doctors and lawyers and retired teachers. The rent was more than fair, this compared to the eight hundred Miles was paying. Eight hundred a month wasn't a lot to shell out for your own slice of sleepy suburbia a few miles outside of downtown Serling Oaks. The far more exquisite two-story that Miles had lived in with Stephanie, and still owned, was a bit closer to town but still on the outskirts, standing in the middle of the winding hill that was Edgebrook Road. That house was in a whole other world. Not the steady quiet of his current address, Edgebrook had a lot of growing families.

Something Miles would never be able to experience.

There were no cars parked out front, nor next to his grey pickup in the driveway. No sign of Jimmy's red truck anywhere. Yet overhead the footsteps continued.

To make sure he wasn't overreacting, Miles stepped out onto the front porch—the thermometer hanging next to his mailbox reading seventy-eight in the balmy shade. To the immediate left of his door was the entrance for his upstairs neighbor. The front door was shut, as was the screen door. A sign was taped up on the inside of the glass, facing out.

FOR RENT
2 BEDROOMS

Scribbled in black Sharpie underneath was Jimmy's cell number.

The bothersome humidity caused Miles to scratch at the irritated skin under his beard while he contemplated his next move. It was possible the vacancy had been filled and he not know of it, but he hadn't seen anyone come by lately or noticed the unmistakable sounds of furniture being carried up the stairwell. Surely he would have heard something before today.

Unless . . .

The notion of a break-in came to mind. Seemed a little far-fetched that someone would break into an obviously empty apartment space where there was nothing of value.

Unless they wanted to hide out. Could be some drugged out homeless guy. Probably saw the FOR RENT sign and thought he struck gold.

That theory didn't hold much water either after a little consideration. By the measure of the steps crossing the floor, whomever was up there wasn't too concerned about being heard.

Plus, looking at the frame near the lock, there were no signs of a forced entry.

"Well, shit."

With the landlady down in Florida until September and her grandson on call but never one to rely on answering a ringing phone, there was always calling the police to check out the second floor, but that was a step Miles was ready to take. That small voice in his head wasn't willing to settle on the idea that what he had heard was real.

Since climbing out of bed he hadn't heard a thing.

There's a way to know for sure.

He had a key.

Two weeks ago, when stopping to collect the rent for June, old Ms. Hutchings had handed over a spare ring with two keys—one for the front door, one for the second floor, which was marked APT2. She gave the instruction that the keys were only to be used in the case of an emergency. He supposed this qualified.

The lock for the handle on the front door turned without a problem but the door itself needed some forcing to open, the wood swollen against the jamb from the sun shining directly on the porch. Miles put his shoulder into the door several times before it gave. A rank smell from the inside hit him like a solid fist. Stale, musty air that had been cooped up inside the stairwell filled his nostrils and brought him to cough. Though unpleasant, the noxious odor of the stagnant air coupled with the door being difficult to open, which suggested it hadn't been opened in some time, put Miles at a conflicted ease. While he wasn't likely facing a break-in, the possibility that his mind fabricated the noises he heard, was no comfort at all.

Before he reached midway up the stairs the fresh air coming in through the screen door had flushed out much of the stink. Each inhale became far more tolerable.

There wasn't much in the way of light on the staircase. The bulb that hung from the exposed beams in the ceiling over the landing at the top had long blown out. The little bit around him he could see was made possible by the sun shining against the open doorway below. What Miles didn't see until it was too late was the spider web stretching wall to wall in front of his face. Once he stripped away and spat out the dusty strands there was nothing between him on the landing and the door marked APT2.

It felt stupid to knock. Also didn't feel right to use the key and barge right in.

Instead he put an ear close enough to listen.

Part of him—the minute part of him that wasn't convinced what he heard hadn't been conjured in his head—wondered how long this was going to go on. There was nothing to hear. No footsteps over the inside floor. No strain of the floorboards. No voices, not even the mild noises of the old house itself. A small sweat broke out in anticipation.

Go ahead, said the voice. *Go on in. See for yourself there's nothing there.*

That little heckling internal voice, the same one that called him crazy for seeing fleeting glimpses of his wife out of the corner of his vision, for talking to her when she wasn't there, had come out shortly after Stephanie was taken from him. While the voice was always nagging, always taunting, it was also a voice of reason. It was never wrong. When it spoke, he listened.

So he tried the key.

The ridges slid fine into the slot of the lock. But there was a problem when Miles tried to turn the key. It wouldn't budge in either direction. There had been no problems before when he went in to scope the layout. The key turned fine then and that was only a month ago. He tried twisting the handle, which moved freely both ways, but the door wouldn't budge. Miles tried the second key, the one for the front door off the porch, and, as expected, that did no good either.

To calm his frustrations, he paused a moment, pinching the spot between his eyes on the bridge of his nose where an ache was forming. He looked at the Master Bolt on the door, then at the keys in his hand. He stuck the one for APT2 back into the keyhole. It went in as it should.

"Okay," he whispered, and attempted a second turn. No dice. The lock refused to slide.

Miles sighed. He pulled out the key. "Forget it."

He turned to go back down the stairs but stopped and tried listening again. Nothing.

The little voice inside him said: *Maybe you should try the key again.*

Back in his own apartment, Miles tossed the keys for APT2 onto the coffee table, went straight for the bathroom, and pulled open the medicine cabinet.

Ah, said the voice. *Your crazy pills.*

The Ambien sat on the left side of the middle shelf. He knew right where they were before the cabinet door opened. His eyes were right on them before they came into view. The large red pills could be seen through the transparent bottle. Half of the prescription remained.

Two will just make you a zombie. How about three?

He shook three of them loose into his palm and dry swallowed them. When he closed the cabinet door, Miles caught his own haggard, exhausted face in the reflection of the mirror. He was disgusted with what he saw so he didn't linger. He went back to his bed and lay staring up at the ceiling, waiting for the pills to put him to sleep. He listened, for any sounds, upstairs or anywhere. The silence of the neighborhood was unnerving. It wasn't like this at the old house, the old neighborhood. End of spring into summer meant family cookouts, adults working in their gardens, music blasting, kids running around the houses, scream-ing in joy, chasing each other, playing games . . . completely unaware how cruel the world around them could be.

These were the sounds Miles wanted to get away from.

Sounds he wished now he could hear again as he drifted off.

Sounds he deeply missed.

An artist often struggles with doubt when attempting to accomplish The Work. This uncertainty in their abilities tends to exist right up to the moment before they begin.

There was only one thing on his mental itinerary to do the entire day and he still managed to be late. On the plus side he awoke refreshed with not a single trace of any visions of dreams knocking around in his thoughts. There was also no phantom touches. What there was instead was a trail of drool leading down the left side of his face, down under his ear, and ending with a damp pool on the sheet under his head. But the undisturbed sleep was what mattered most.

In the beginning, after Stephanie was gone, he dreamt all the time. He saw his wife around every corner of their house, behind him in every mirror. The photos on the walls didn't help the pangs of his grief. But he couldn't do anything about them, couldn't bring himself to take down every hanging picture and stuff them away in boxes. If he removed everything that reminded him of his late wife, the house would be bare.

He also couldn't work.

Work meant moving on. Moving on meant putting it behind him. He wasn't ready.

But not working also meant he was just existing in the house, nothing to comfort him but the loneliness, the sounds of happy families surrounding him in the neighborhood, and the thoughts in his head—the taunting voice that manifested itself as his perfect foil.

He resisted the meds at first, when Andrews wanted to prescribe them, thinking instead that a new environment might do the trick. Miles couldn't bear the thought of selling the house, but he had also come to terms with the fact that he had to get out. Fortunately he owned it free and clear so it could just sit as he looked for a place.

The search wasn't a long one because he wasn't overly picky. He just wanted to get away and hope nothing of his troubles would follow.

But on the first night in the apartment, having been a widower less than four weeks, he had a dream. One of the most vivid he had experienced, up to that time.

He was back in the lounge of the old Sunset Moon Café. He was there, sipping nervously at a cup of coffee, just minutes before she would walk through the door for the very first time. The dream played all the beats exactly as they happened. Every detail culled from the recesses of his memory and realized, right down to the hollow tunes of light jazz in the air.

He sat at a small black table with four chairs, none of them matching. The walls were papered with random band fliers and announcements for poet jams taped up next to and even overlapping one another. The interior walls of the Sunset Moon had been a billboard for artists and events past and future. The modern day bohemian coffeehouse, settled on the upper mainline drag, was once an original, raw, and refreshing take on the moody blues atmosphere that attracted college students of all types. The style of which has been copycatted in many small town hippy cafés since the turn of the century. Intimate places such as these, places occupied on weekend nights by caffeine-addicted young adults reciting long-winded beverage orders and stoned out coeds debating current issues on old ratty sofas, were once cool.

On this wintry afternoon thirteen years ago, Miles sat with a fresh mug of Jamaican-Me-Crazy that was both keeping his hands warm and working to put his jangled nerves at ease.

There was plenty to admire about the décor and plenty to enjoy about listening to the acoustic strumming of a pained, raspy artist on the verge of discovery as her smoky lyrics filled the rooms through the antique sound system. But these things didn't even register on his radar. His heart was too busy filling his ears with nervous, incessant throbs. His eyes too busy scanning passersby out the storefront window. All the while wondering if this girl would show.

He took a cautious sip from the mug. The bitterness infused with rich coconut swam past his tongue and down into his belly, leaving a warm trail in its wake. His stomach responded with a nervous flutter. Miles straightened up in his seat with bated breath when two people walked in front of the large picture window from the right. He relaxed somewhat when he realized both were in fact male—their feminine walk, caked on eye makeup, and shoulder-length hair threw him off.

From his seat at the table in the lounge area, looking out over a small stretch of Main Street going east, he had the advantage of a view leading up to the café's front door. He would be able to see her before she saw him.

If she showed.

She said she would be there. He looked around for a clock on the wall and found one. There was a Monkeys Typing band sticker over the bottom half but he could see she was now eight minutes late.

Outside there rose a blustery spike of wind. Snowflakes scattered through the air. Some even brushed the glass and melted down to droplets in seconds. It was when the gust settled that the next form walked passed the window. He recognized her in that very instant. Though her face was obscured by a violet scarf and her long hair trailed behind her in the chilly breeze, she stood out against the grey gloom of the day by her white coat. It was a soft white, not a speck of dirt tarnished the fabric. Behind her the tail of the coat billowed out, revealing nylon-covered legs that were tucked into black winter boots.

He stood up without realizing.

Stephanie.

He didn't feel his legs carry him into the adjacent room where she would come inside. The door opened and he felt the cold sting from outside prickle his naked jaw. Flakes of melting snow disintegrated in her hair. She unwrapped the scarf to reveal a long, slender neck that was featureless with the exception of a small round birthmark next to her throat.

She was looking for him. Prior to this she had only seen a single image of him—the one he had posted on his profile page at LocalSingles. She had put up two.

Those precious few seconds before she spotted him he spent admiring her. Feeling the change in the wind that preceded her. On some subconscious level it was like he was aware of the dream. Aware that he was first looking upon the girl he would fall deeply in love with and later marry. Aware that eventually he was going to lose a big part of himself because he was going to lose her.

That she was destined to be murdered.

She found him and a smile brightened her wind-burnt cheeks. He walked up to meet her.

"Stephanie?"

A prickling of nerves ignited in his belly.

"Hi," she said, warmly. There was no hint she had been suffering from the same swarm of butterflies in her stomach as he.

Miles couldn't help it—his eyes took the long journey all the way up and down her. He tried not to be so overt. "You look . . . (he wanted to say *amazing, gorgeous, beautiful, incredibly fuckable,* but wisely settled on) . . . very nice."

Truth was there wasn't much of her to see. The long white coat was belted closed, forcing his imagination to picture the shapes and curves underneath. Northeast winters were known for their brutality, and were especially so when it came to a young man trying to capture any glimpse he could otherwise manage in much fairer weather. If he wanted to check out wind-chapped cheekbones, however, he was getting a gratuitous eye full.

At the counter they were greeted by a young female barista with a nametag reading Jo whose style fit the tone of the place. Her black hair had intermittent streaks of purple. Both of Jo's arms were sleeved in tattoos. And every available hole in her head featured at least one gauge or piercing. "You guys know what you want?"

They put in their orders: a tall whipped peppermint mocha cappuccino for him; a grande lean cinnamon chai latte for her. The raven-haired Jo scribbled it all down on a Post-It pad in a messy shorthand that only she seemed able to decipher and set off to fix their drinks.

Miles asked, "So how was your day?"

"It's Friday," Stephanie said with a tired sigh, "so I guess it couldn't be all *that* bad, right?"

"Doesn't sound like it was all *that* good, either."

She explained, "I love teaching, don't get me wrong. It's not always easy or fun, but at least the kids make it enjoyable. Raising these parents though, *that's* tough work."

The cappuccino machine hissed loudly, making talking at normal volumes difficult. Jo grated sticks of cinnamon over the steaming glass of chai. She finished off the decorative touches on both drinks and set them on the counter.

There were rows empty tables in by the stage, where the lighting was a touch more intimate. They picked a spot near the front corner of the room. The music in the café changed over to a pluck-n-drum jazz beat. The twangy voice coming through the speaker was that of an older gentleman, wailing on about a list of things in his life he'd been "missin'."

"How long have you been teaching?" Miles asked. On his way to the Sunset Moon that afternoon he tried not to overthink it. He was worried he'd run out of things to talk about. He never did well in a pinch so he prepped himself with questions to ask to keep her talking. Silence was a slow death in the dating department.

Stephanie mulled over the question while blowing gently on her chai. "This is my . . . fourth year in primary. First year teaching Kindergarten."

"You always wanted to be a teacher?"

She nodded, took a cautious sip. "Staying in primary or intermediate is not something I want to do forever. Actually, I would love to take a few more classes to get my PhD and then get into a state college where I can be a Lit professor. The thought of lecturing in one of those big halls with hundreds of students, preaching the words and themes of history's great pieces of fiction, spending my Sunday evenings curled up on the couch grading papers about Hemmingway and Twain in comparison to today's Rowling and Nicholas Sparks . . . But . . . I think for the foreseeable future, my days will be spent among nose-pickers and paste eaters, and my Sunday evenings getting caught up on The Amazing Race."

"Nothing wrong with that." He sipped his mocha. "What's stopping you from going back to school for your PhD?"

She took another careful sip of her tea. "About forty grand in student loans I need to pay down." She said this with a laugh, and when he heard her laugh for the first time it aroused those butterflies in his belly. After she set her glass down she adjusted in the seat, leaning against the backing and crossing one leg over the other knee. He liked seeing her get comfortable. It said things were going well, that she wasn't looking for an exit strategy.

"Art school cost me about the same," said Miles.

"Oh yeah, I saw that your profile said Artist. I should tell you I've got a few artists in my classroom that can do some pretty amazing things with finger-paints."

Miles enjoyed her sense of humor. It did wonders to set him at ease.

Stephanie asked, "Working on anything right now?"

"I'm actually waiting to hear back from a small production company in Philadelphia about some concepts I sent them."

"Do you sketch? Paint?"

"Both."

"So you design logos for companies . . . ?"

"I make movie posters."

By the tilt of her head it wasn't what she was expecting. "Oh." Then came the usual response he got when telling people what he did for a living. "Those aren't all done on computers?"

"Many are," he said. "But then there are those, like me, who still work with brushes and paint and different kinds of pencils."

She seemed impressed.

"You must be very good. Tell me a movie you did a poster for. Maybe I'll know it."

He gave her the title of a recent romance story that starred Richard Gere.

"Yes, I know that one!" she said. "I went with a friend to see it. We thought the movie kinda sucked but I'm sure your poster was great."

They shared a laugh in the beginning of a long moment where neither of them said another word. He just kept looking at her, her staring back. The sparkles of light glimmering in her eyes were like moonbeams off the ocean. They didn't need words.

For seemingly no reason, this is when he awoke. It was the onset of dawn on his first morning in the apartment. The transition was jarring. He'd just been with her, taking in the glimmer of her stare, admiring the smile lines in her face—a slightly younger face—and then his eyes opened in the deep violet light of dawn bleeding in through the windows.

Back then he awoke to nothing more than a faint remembrance of what he had dreamt.

As he lay there now, rested and, thanks to his pills, clearheaded without the tendrils of a dream latched into his mind, it dawned on him that he was lying the same way as when he had awakened on that first morning. Looking at the ceiling.

This reminded him. He had a phone call to make. Two, actually.

By the clock on his dresser he was supposed to be sitting in Applebees down the parkway in eight minutes. He was stripping down on his way to the bathroom, cell phone in hand. He put the first call on speaker and set the phone down on the sink while struggling with his socks.

Bryan, his agent, answered. "You better not be cancellin' on me, or I'm gonna come over there and kick your ass."

"I'm just running a little late. On my way out the door now." Miles could hear the light commotion of a busy lunch crowd in the background. Bryan didn't sound too happy to have to wait a little bit longer, but, what else was he going to do.

"You're lucky I like you," said Bryan.

"You're lucky I've made you a lot of money," Miles replied.

"That goes both ways," Bryan said with a husky laugh. "Sounds like you just woke up."

Miles hit END on the phone's touchscreen.

He next fought to get his pants off while waiting on the second call to be answered. But it rang through right to voicemail. The recording of his landlady's gravely smoker's voice instructed him to leave a brief message and a number so she would call back.

"Hey Gloria, it's Miles, you're favorite tenant. Listen I was just calling to let you know I've been hearing some noises upstairs . . . didn't know if maybe you'd rented it out or not. Sounds like someone's moving around up there. Anyway, no rush, just give me a call when you can. Hope you're—"

He was interrupted by a series of beeps indicating he'd run out of time leaving his message. The call disconnected.

He put the phone back on the sink and dropped his paisley blue boxers to the tiled floor at his feet. He was tempted to forgo the shower and just change so he could get out faster. Then he sniffed his under arms.

He would need a shower.

Time dedicated to a drawing can never be underestimated nor overlooked. It is only when committed to The Work that the artist begins to determine and understand the length of their sacrifice.

"There he is."

Flashing a toothy grin that was obscenely white, a burly man in a navy pinstripe suit and jet black spiky hair with sunglasses resting on his forehead shifted his way out from the booth as he caught glimpse of Miles, who arrived thirty-three minutes late. Miles had been in such a hurry getting dressed and getting out of the apartment that if not for the sharp breeze that hit him while crossing the parking lot into Applebees, he wouldn't have otherwise noticed his fly was down.

Before Miles could fully extend his hand in reach for a modest shake, Bryan was already spreading his large arms wide, showing his enormous wingspan. "Bring it on in, brother."

Bryan pulled him in for a tight squeeze, picking him up and growling like a bear, garnering a few crooked eyebrows from nearby tables. "Damn it's good to see you, man."

"Likewise," Miles said, straining for breath against the strength in Bryan's arms wrapped around him, as well as the strength of the Axe body spray he had doused himself with. They took their seats in the booth. In front of Bryan was a half-drained beer, the foam long gone, the glass sweaty. "Startin' a little early?"

"Just warmin' up waitin' for you, homes." Homes. Typical Bryan. "Jesus, before you called I thought you were gonna stand me up. I was lookin' all pathetic sittin' here by myself."

"Oh come on," said Miles. "You're giving yourself too much credit; you were pathetic long before this."

"That may be, and Molly may agree with you," Bryan said. He took a long gulp, emptying the pilsner, and leaned back against the red leather cushions, spreading his arms out across the backing. "But it's barely after noon on a gorgeous day and I could've sworn on the phone that it sounded like you'd been nappin' it all away."

Miles sighed, there was no use hiding it. "If you *must* know, I didn't sleep well at all last night." He wasn't about to delve into the details, like mentioning the dream he had and the strange feeling he awoke to, but hoped offering up a little something would get Bryan past this and onto the next topic, hopefully getting down to why Bryan had called for this lunch meeting a week ago. "So I popped a few of my meds and caught up on a few hours. No biggie."

"Those the meds the therapist put you on?"

Miles already regretted saying too much. "Yes."

"Are they helpin'?"

Fortunately for Miles they were interrupted when a waitress stopped by to ask if he wanted something to drink. He considered something strong to get him through this lunch but, in the end, opted for iced tea. Bryan nodded when asked about a refill. When the waitress went off, Bryan resumed his questioning.

"How come you're not sleepin' well?"

Miles shrugged. "Just a lot on my mind, I guess."

A sly grin crept up on Bryan's face. He leaned in, interested, setting both forearms on the edge of the table. "By chance would any of this thinkin' be about you maybe comin' out of your retirement?"

Miles gave him a funny look. "You wish."

"You know what, Miles? You're right. I do." Bryan licked his bottom lip as if he had been savoring what he was about to say. "It's been way too long. And you're gonna sit there and tell me that since we last spoke—which was like what, February?—that not a single idea for a new picture, a sketch, hell even the thought of a napkin doodle has crossed your mind?"

"Nada," Miles said with a shake of his head. "What can I tell you man, the well's all dried up."

"I hope that's not the permanent case, Miles."

"Why do you say that?"

At first Bryan seemed hesitant to say, but did so regardless. "Because the last thing I want for you is to keep goin' on with this . . . this . . . erectile dysfunction for artists."

"Erectile dysfunction?" Miles snorted. "That was the best description you could come up with?"

"Isn't that kinda what it is?"

Miles frowned. "You think Molly will be upset if you lend me some of your pills to help out with that?"

Bryan ignored his snide remark. "Actually, my friend, I may have just what you need."

Before he could elaborate, the waitress was back at their table, drinks in hand.

"Everybody know what they want?" She wasn't holding a pad or pen, just waited, eyes switching back and forth to see who would go first, ready to commit their orders to memory. Miles went with the Chicken Caesar Salad. Bryan ordered a dozen boneless wings. Extra blue cheese.

"God, I love their boneless wings," Bryan said after the waitress left. "Molly's got us on this special diet and I can't tell you how long it's been since I've had any *real* food. The wings are the only reason I decided on comin' here today. Look at me, I'm already salivatin' all over myself."

Miles crossed his arms. "So coming here today had nothing to do with me?"

"Miles, I assure you, this is absolutely all about you." A beat. There was hesitance scrawled across Bryan's face. Something he wasn't saying. Something he appeared conflicted about.

"What is it?" Miles asked.

Bryan made an uncomfortable shift in his seat. He sighed and lowered his voice. "All right, Miles, listen. For the next few minutes, I'm gonna speak to you as your agent, all right, not as your friend, not as your brother-in-law. This is a business meeting after all."

Miles asked, "Are we technically still considered brothers-in-law? Or would it be brother-in-laws?"

Not even a glimmer of a reaction from his agent. "You'll always be family to me, Miles, no matter what's official or not. Know that. But what I'm gonna tell you . . . it ain't easy for me. Know that, too."

Like an old car trying to start, Bryan stalled a few times trying to get out whatever was on his mind. Whatever words that'd formed in his head clung to his lips flapping open and closed with each false start. Miles reassured him that it was fine, just say it already. Bryan remained apprehensive, but finally managed to get beyond his own reluctance.

"Look at you, Miles."

The left eyebrow on Miles's forehead sprouted up as he cocked his head just slightly at an angle, like a dog would when unsure of the noise they just heard. "Oh," he said, "this oughta be good."

"I mean, no offense or anything."

"No, not at all. Don't worry about it." Miles settled back into the cushion of the seat and further awaited the bludgeoning. "How could I get upset if you said 'no offense,' right?"

"Remember, I'm saying all of this as your agent."

Miles wound his hand in a gesture that said *let's go already.*

"Honestly," said Bryan, his eyes wincing, "you look like hell, man."

A sardonic smile spread across Miles's face. Not as bad as he expected. "And there it is. See, was that so hard?"

"Actually, you look worse than hell; you look like you were hawked up the throat of hell and spit out on the ground."

Miles considered this critique. "That's colorful."

Bryan didn't placate to the sarcasm. He went on with his list of faults because he already had a mind to, ticking them off one by one. Each obviously well thought out long before either of them arrived for this lunch. "You've got this scraggily, homeless man beard, which is fine, I get it—it kinda goes along with the whole starvin' artist look. Except you're obviously not starvin' because you've got this . . . little . . ."—he placed his hands on his own protruding gut—"paunch, do you follow me?"

Miles blinked, feigning astonishment. "I'm fat?"

"You've put on a little weight, bro. Plus you're pale like a goddamn vampire. It's almost summer, man! Have you been out in the sun at all? Not to mention, beyond everythin' I just said, you're not workin', or even thinkin' about workin' on anythin' new."

When it seemed his brother-in-law agent was finished hitting the bullets on his list, Miles gave a retort in the only way he knew how. "Wait. *You're* calling *me* fat?"

Bryan huffed in frustration. "Goddamnit, Miles, I'm being serious here."

For the sake of his brother-in-law's growing exasperation, not to mention taking a moment to consider how difficult it must've been for Bryan to be so open and bring all of this up, Miles reeled in his mocking defensiveness. He proceeded to convey himself genuinely because of the love and respect he had for the man across from him. "Look, I appreciate it, Bry. I appreciate you looking out for me. Really. I do. All kidding aside, I think it's sweet that you're worried. But you don't need to.

"The beard . . . I've just never worn one. You know how much your sister hated even feeling the slightest bit of stubble on my face. She once told me that I could grow the hair on my face if she could grow the hair on her legs."

Bryan grinned. "Molly said that to me once. 'Cept it wasn't my face and it wasn't her legs."

Miles winced and decided not to ask. "Yeah, well, anyway, I know I'm a little overweight. I'm gonna work on that. It's just . . . things got tough for a while and these pills I'm on aren't helping with the weight. You of all people should know how hard things have been."

"I do, man." Bryan sighed. His eyes lowered to his refilled beer, which he had yet to even taste. The glass was heavily sweating, leaving a thick watery outline of the circular mug on the wooden tabletop. "I do."

The quiet that snuck in between them felt like a momentary silence out of respect for Stephanie. Her death had hit them both hard. Bryan just managed to bounce back faster after losing his sister. He had reasons to pull himself back up. He had a family at home to hold and bury his tears in, whose strength he could rely on when his own was fading. A wonderful wife and two girls was enough to awaken him and encourage him to drag himself out of the hole filled with sorrows. A hole Miles still occasionally found himself standing in with no one around to offer a hand, no one to even distract him, no one to fill the empty place that his wife had filled for twelve years. Just him, alone in the hole that had only grown deeper since that day in September. The sides all around him were muddied and soft—trying to get out too fast by himself only resulted in sinking deeper.

But he was still standing.

"Maybe you could at least get out in the sun a little," Bryan said. "Hibernatin' season's over. Get some color on those cheeks. Go for walks or something—that'll help with the weight."

"The Scottish in me hates the sun," Miles said. "I don't even tan. I burn and just go back to white."

"Well then," Bryan said, folding his hands on the tabletop, "how about we just get down to why I asked you here today?"

Surprise lit up Miles's face. "You mean this all wasn't just a touching breakdown of my faults?"

"Hardly." Bryan cleared his throat, ready to get down to business. A little rejuvenation of excitement slipped back into his face and voice. "What if I told you, Miles, that I booked you a gig?"

The complete opposite of his glowing agent, Miles just stared back, unblinking, blank. Bryan gave some time to spot a reaction. None came.

"I can't tell if you're excited," Bryan said. "It's nothing big, just an in during the Art Walk for July."

Miles continued to sit quiet, motionless. His bottom lip may have drooped a bit; his jaw slowly coming unhinged. On the inside it was a completely different matter. His heart was making quite a racket, drumming away wildly through the canals of his ears, a relentless rise in beats. Against his chest and his ribs he could feel it throbbing, threatening to burst out of his body. The rising angst left his throat dry. Finally, he said: "I can't tell if you're serious."

"Serious as a heart attack, Miles."

Terrible choice of words.

There was no wink, no smile or nudge, no giveaway that Miles could see—though he hoped, prayed even—that this was all just part of Bryan's terrible sense of humor. Troubling thing was, when it came to business, Bryan was never one to mess around with getting a client booked. He prided himself on his successes. And why not—he was good at his job. Which never worried Miles before, but had him stunned now.

"Why didn't you ask me first?" Miles said. "As a client of yours, it would have been nice to get a heads up long before you had this brilliant idea that included putting me in front of hundreds of people at an art show."

Bryan corrected, "Exhibition. You wouldn't even have to say anything if you didn't want to. It's a small deal and setup." Then he lowered his eyes to the beer glass, his enthusiasm dropping a few notches, his tone a bit more directed. "And to answer your question in two ways: this is your heads up, and because I knew you'd say no."

Miles closed his eyes and sighed inward. He removed his glasses and rubbed his temples as if it were all some bad dream he could pull himself away from.

Bryan asked, "What would your therapist say?"

"Andrews?" Miles spent the next few seconds pondering a lie. "He'd say it was too soon. He would say you should have asked me first."

A scrunch of Bryan's face said he wasn't buying that. "I think he'd say this is a wonderful chance, Miles, to get yourself back out there."

"Well, good thing we're not asking him."

"When do you see him again?"

"Tomorrow."

"You should talk to him about it, Miles. Like I said, it's not a big deal. It's a forty-five minute obligation on a Friday night. Plus, it's the Garland Gallery, so you're guaranteed eyes on your work."

To all of this Miles held up a finger in protest. "Uh, nay. It's a forty-five minute obligation *next* Friday night. It's also not just a forty-five minute obligation. You know how these things go. Maybe I don't have to talk for half an hour but there're meet-and-greets, handshakes, introductions, endless amounts of schmoozing—oh, not the least of which, *artwork*. It's the fucking Garland Gallery, Bry! I can't just hang some old pieces. There has to be something to display."

Concerned eyes reared their way at the rise in Miles's voice. The most concern came from a table of two parents with their three children, all of whom were peeking over the back of their booth. All of them wide-eyed at his use of the f-word. A flare of heat that was agitation mixed with embarrassment rose through Miles's face.

"That's the point, Miles." Bryan spoke low and calm. "And there *will* be art on the walls. Yours."

"Yeah? And where are you gonna get that from? I already said it: the well's dry. I've done next to nothing in nine months."

"So you just gotta find some inspiration is all."

"Oh yeah, that's it." Miles snapped his fingers. "Just as easy as that, huh?"

Bryan huffed, obviously bothered his good news wasn't better received. "I'm just trying to help you, Miles. I know how it's been." He then asked, "There isn't anything you have that no one's seen before? Nothing at the house?"

Miles took a breath and tried to relax. He knew Bryan was just trying to do good by him and had to keep it in mind as their conversation continued. "Just the private stuff and any works-in-progress in the studio, but . . . I haven't stepped foot in there since . . . well, that night." He didn't have to say any more for Bryan to know those pieces were off limits.

"Have you been back there?" Bryan asked of the house.

Miles didn't look up. "Usually at the end of the month I stop by for the mail. I don't get out though, just pull up to the mailbox. I haven't been inside since I got the last of my things into the apartment."

Bryan went for his beer, but then it looked like he didn't want it. "How long are you going to be able to afford two places?"

"Way I figured it . . . if my investments tank . . . about two years at the most. House was paid off long ago. The bills every month aren't that much. Taxes aren't bad." He shrugged. "If my investments continue to gain . . . I may never have to go back."

Seeming impressed at how protected his client was, Bryan rubbed his jaw and gave an approving nod. Miles expected him to say something about how stupid it was choosing to pay eight hundred a month to live in a small duplex in the suburbs compared to the beautiful, spacious— and *paid for*—two-story home on the wealthy lane of Edgebrook Road. It wouldn't be the first time this conversation ran its course. But Bryan remained mum on the subject. Thankfully.

"Listen, Miles. The last thing I wanted to do was get you all worked up into a tizzy. Just last week I had lunch with a friend who works at the Garland. She mentioned the featured artist for July backed out—had double-booked himself somehow. Anyway, that's not what's important here. She asked if I knew anyone she could go back and tell the owner about. You were the first I thought of."

Miles scoffed. "Lucky me."

"Yeah lucky you—you need this, man." Bryan slid his untouched beer away from in front of him and folded his arms on the table. "I didn't go in there begging for you. I haven't tried to get you anything anywhere for the last nine months. Because I know, Miles. I've respected your want for nothing." He paused. "I have."

"I know."

"But you need this. Because at some point you've got to make a choice.

You've got to decide soon whether or not to pull yourself all the way back up. Or else you'll never get to your feet again." Bryan's eyes watered a bit. "After Steph . . . I became so depressed it almost ruined my marriage. I've seen what's happened to you, and I can't watch it anymore. It's like slowly watching your favorite pet just curl up in a corner waiting to die."

Miles folded his arms. "You're comparing me to your childhood hamster?"

"Think about it, man, what would Steph want you to do?"

Bryan may not have known but Miles asked himself that question many times. And he never liked the answer. If she had known he'd allowed himself to get to the point he was at . . .

"Now, it's nothing upscale. You know, you've been there before. The Garland is probably the nicest gallery we have here. It's not the Agora, and it's nowhere near the Christopher Henry. The Art Walk is just one of those monthly hometown events that's just as much about getting the people out and getting them to spend bucks on overpriced food and getting them to step inside places and shops they normally wouldn't than it is about the art displays themselves. You may get fifty people, at most a hundred to pass through. It's not a huge commitment, other than the pieces for display, but I have faith that you'll think of something." Bryan leaned in with a pleading face. "Come on, Miles, what do ya say? They're desperate. I'm desperate. You . . . Well . . . Don't make me go back and tell them they don't have an artist."

"Everyone's desperate," Miles said. "That's welcoming."

"All right, they want you, Miles. I was being facetious to lighten the pressure on you. Now, come on, what's it gonna be?"

As much as Miles and his spiked anxiety wanted to decline in the most kind and professional way, there was a small part of him, that voice of reason, speaking out. It repeated Bryan's earlier question.

What would Steph want you to do?

It wasn't so easy to decline after all.

In his head only, Miles began to entertain the thought that if there were ever an opportunity to wade back into the art scene, there were fewer intimidating scenarios in the world than the monthly Serling Oaks Art Walk. His brother-in-law was right: Miles wouldn't have to entertain the masses, just a few dozen townies who would wander in off the street after chowing down on cheap vendor meals or overpriced Mediterranean and looking to walk off the calories. There would be a lot of families—a lot of kids who wouldn't know his name because his face wasn't immediately recognizable. But the point would be to make a slow reappearance. Get his name back out there. Gauge people's interest in him, in his work.

"Let's say, just for a second, that I go along with this."

Bryan nodded along and seemed to lick the corners of his mouth.

Miles continued, couldn't believe he was actually saying it. "I've seen the place, I know the setup. I would need something like . . . eight pieces to go on their walls. Fifteen at the most and that's if I go with smaller canvases."

"No need to overwork yourself," said Bryan, keeping everything in measure, surely happy enough Miles was even considering the chance at all. "Just stick to eight, focus on that. It's a good, even number. Not too tall an order and nothin' to wag a finger at either."

Such an ass-kisser when you wanna be. Miles almost smirked at the thought. "But I only have a week. In the last eight months I haven't managed so much as a doodle on a grocery list, so I wanna know I have an out here."

"Don't you have a finished piece already?" Bryan asked. "I thought you did a painting around the time you moved into the apartment?"

Miles had long tried to forget about that one. The oil painting was the first piece of art he attempted after Stephanie, a desperate time when nothing was coming to mind. It was like he had developed a form of writer's block for artists (writer's block . . . a much better way to describe his condition rather than Bryan's diagnosis of erectile dysfunction). The result of his first picture had been a face surrounded by butterflies, but a face that wasn't his wife's. Like a snap from an old Polaroid camera, a flash had gone off in his brain the first night he spent in the apartment. The night had just quieted down, all of his stuff was moved in, when it happened. What he could see in his head was something that felt so close but he couldn't touch it. Quickly, like any thought being grasped at, the vision became distant. The only way he could think to capture it was to draw it out and fill the canvas with what colors he'd brought.

The intense focus instilled in him in those late hours was nothing he experienced before, even when forced to balance numerous projects during the midst of his lightning hot career. It's also something he hadn't experienced since. The drought continued right after he went to bed that night, when he dreamt of that wintry afternoon at the Sunset Moon Café.

But with that one painting, a long and quiet guilt set in the morning after it was finished. Hope throughout had been that this was his path to healing, but when Miles found himself expressing such heated emotions towards the face—a female face—and all the desire it brought out in him, he decided to abandon it, and bury it somewhere he wouldn't have to see it.

"I don't know what happened to that one," he lied. "I would have to do eight pictures."

Bryan smiled. "And no worries. If something happens and you don't have the eight, I'll just tell them you got food poisoning."

"And speaking of which," said Miles. They both glanced up as their waitress returned, carrying a large tray with their lunches on her shoulder.

After they were served Bryan choked down his beer (the bitterness hitting him hard now that it wasn't ice cold anymore), while Miles examined the mound of lettuce and croutons buried beneath a thick slopping of Caesar dressing. The strips of grilled chicken were discovered and excavated much like buried fossils after much sifting. The salad felt limp and unappealing against the touch of his fork. Meanwhile, Bryan dug into his zesty boneless wings, cutting up the remaining eleven after sticking the first one whole into his mouth. With each cut the tender meat on the inside released a cloud of steam and an enticing aroma into the air.

"They do look good," Miles observed.

Bryan forked more into his waiting mouth. "You've never had them?"

Miles shook his head. "You mind if I try one?"

His brother-in-law didn't bother waiting until he swallowed, talking as he chomped away. Greasy splotches of barbeque and bleu cheese stained his bottom lip and chin. "Miles, I'm allowed thirteen hundred calories a day. Tonight, for dinner, Molly's making stuffed red peppers with brown rice. I'd rather eat whatever the baby's gonna get. So yeah, I mind."

Miles spoke in a luring tone. "What if I said I would definitely do the Art Walk?"

Bryan stopped chewing. His eyes narrowed and he revealed a face that said he wanted to either argue or curse—his artery clogging lunch meant that much to him. "That's petty, Miles, even for you." He then proceeded to fork over the pieces of two boneless wings onto Miles's plate. "There," he said. "We're even."

Their lunch resumed. And though Miles went into their meeting not wanting to discuss anything too personal, he couldn't help his own curiosity. He hoped Bryan wouldn't call him on the hypocrisy. "So," he said, after wiping bleu cheese off his mouth, "how are Molly and the kids?"

For a brief speck of a moment, when Bryan's eyes flicked up in question, he did seem to take note of the shift in their conversation. Still, for his own reasons, he let it go and humored Miles. "They're good. They're all good. Lily just started walking. Funny now she was crawling a few months ago and Molly and I could still watch TV and keep an eye on her. Now, once we look away, she's gone. Just like her sister was. That kid never liked to stay in one place for too long either. Now that Lily's able to get up and move on her own, forget about it."

Miles nodded. "Sounds like she's keepin' you busy."

"I tell you, Miles, it's a thing just to keep up with all the stuff: baby locks for the cabinets, baby gates for the stairs, covers for the sockets— we never had these kinds of things growing up and look how we turned out. I don't even know if we had all this stuff for Myra things have changed so fast."

"How is Myra?" Miles asked.

"Doing awesome; right now she's away at cheerleading camp till the end of July. Can't believe she'll be starting middle school in the fall."

"You don't sound too excited about that."

If he had any reservations discussing his life when Miles was being selective about sharing his own, Bryan kept up a good poker face and continued to play the hand dealt. In fact, Miles noted the tough exterior of Bryan Kessler soften and relax while discussing how his girls were changing before his eyes, his posture sagging instead of being so rigid. His hands went up in a powerless gesture of surrender that said *What can I do about it?* "She may be eleven," he said, "but she's still my baby, and she was first. You were never a parent, Mi—" That softened look turned into instant shock then became apologetic really quick at the realization of what just came out of his mouth. "Oh, God, Miles . . . I'm . . ."

Miles waved it off. Turned out he could keep a good poker face as well and not show the sting he just felt. "It's fine. Really. I know what you mean."

Still, there was a long awkward pause that swept over their booth like a shadow. The waitress came back to check on them. Both just nodded that everything was good. After she was gone again neither showed much interest in anything other than the half-eaten meals in front of them.

Finally, Bryan spoke up. "So, yeah, the family's doing great."

"That's good."

"They miss you."

Miles took a long pull off his iced tea.

"*I* miss you, man," said Bryan.

Miles looked into the genuine eyes of his brother-in-law. Large blue eyes—same shade as his younger sister—that were full of regret. "I miss you guys, too."

They finished their lunches in quiet.

Even when painting an artist will always start The Work with a pencil, one with a soft, light weight graphite (6H is good, 4H is better). The lighter the pencil, the easier to erase mistakes. There are always mistakes.

With a clear vision, the artist sits down in front of a blank surface and begins.

Eight drawings. Shit. With the exception of a discarded and buried painting there hadn't been a lick of creativity in the last nine months. This dry spell could have continued for God knows how long, but now he found himself in a wicked tight spot. Eight drawings. Eight drawings and seven days to dig deep and, with any luck, rediscover amongst his dormancy even a shadow of the artist he once was. He supposed if he couldn't drudge up the determination to find it within himself before, what was more inspiring than a deadline?

Following a hug from Bryan and a promise to be in touch soon, Miles left their meeting with the backs of his knees not only sweating but feeling a little lighter, hollowed out almost, as he made a slow walk across the parking lot. His feet, he swore, were floating an inch over the sunlit macadam. He didn't feel in control of his motion, or in his direction; he just happened to be going in the right path toward his silver pickup. The combination of euphoria and nerves cradled in the knot of his stomach brought to the surface a nervous series of burps that allowed him to taste his lunch numerous times over.

Surprisingly, he found, surging along with all of this uncertainty keeping him on edge, there was also a measurable amount of excitement going along with the fact that, soon, he would be getting back to work. Like riding a bicycle, you never unlearned it, you never lost the ability; you were just unsure of your balance until you got back on the seat and started to coast. This was all well and good, except that Miles never learned to ride a bike in the first place.

But you have *drawn and painted before, haven't you? You don't really forget how to move a pencil in your hand.*

Before climbing into the truck, Miles assured himself he would be just fine. The voice in his head told him he would be just fine. The hard part would be getting past the point of beginning. Beginnings were always the most intimidating. Beginnings were where doubts lived, where uncertainties wielded power.

Where a looming, oppressive guilt said he was still too deep in grieving to go back to the normalcies of life. Especially the facets he once enjoyed with his wife around.

Mere milestones to pass.

Miles cranked the ignition, mumbling through the engine turning over that he'd have to take it one step, one picture at a time. And before getting too worked up about the whole situation, the simple reality was that all the prestige and angst and excitement of an art show all boiled down to being within his control. To get started what he needed was an idea. Without an idea for a picture all this planning and scheduling between Bryan and the Garland Gallery was meaningless. The idea was key.

At the same time, Miles realized he couldn't afford the luxury of being too picky. In the past, when he proved far more prolific, any old thought that would encourage a sketch wasn't enough. Those kinds of thoughts came all the time, and time was what ended up being wasted pursuing every single idea that dawned on him. So instead of chewing up precious time making a bunch of sketches where most would later be sifted out before being shown to clients, Miles kept a system of notes, waiting to see which one stood out, which one kept knocking around and growing in his head. The one that refused to be confined to a list and compared, and ignored.

But eight pictures in a week? He needed every idea he could get.

The search for motivation began in his return trip back up the parkway. He scanned the roadsides on both sides of the median, though there wasn't much to get excited about between the steady stream pedestrians entering and exiting the duel Dairy Queen and A&W on their lunch, or the expansive used car lot at Planet Pre-Owned.

Beyond the short stretch of fast food eateries, dingy outlets where more storefronts were dark and empty than not, and enough used car lots where either sales flags were flying or inflatable tube men waved, came a short strip of tall, dense oaks running parallel to the parkway.

Miles felt hardly inspired by any of it. Mostly because he knew he was searching for something to settle on. Settling was the worst, and going around trying to find motivation was almost just as bad. It meant he was out of fresh ideas. He used to loathe those who sat in the middle of a park sketching trees or painting the sky. It meant they settled on something given to them—copying what already existed, what was already created for them, rather than take a chance on being inventive. Anyone with modest art skills could copy scenery. Any amateur could drive around trying to find something to catch their eye. And he hated that he was doing exactly that. Ideas—good ideas—had to come organically.

The idea was the key.

No pressure, said the internal voice of reason. *It's not like you have anything better to do than sit in your apartment and wait for the perfect idea to strike. Isn't The View on in twenty minutes?*

Two blocks from the apartment the light at the intersection for the left turn across the northbound lanes went red. Miles stopped and rubbed at his temples, trying to will away the remnant echo of the condescending voice in his head.

Certainly he did more than just absorb hours of mindless television every day. There was the radio, and a few books he'd been slowly making his way through. Reading hadn't always been his thing but when you're not working there are a lot more hours in a day to fill. He walked, too. Walked a lot, actually. By his inflated middle you'd never guess he put in an average of two miles per day by going around the winding streets near the apartment. So it's not like he did nothing.

Yeah but you've been in a holding pattern, the voice pointed out, refusing to be ignored or quieted. *Maybe this gig is exactly what you've been waiting for.*

Except he hadn't been waiting for anything.

Had he?

Something—a shadow of some kind—crossed over his eyes.

The insect, wings fluttering rapidly, skittered over the outside of his windshield. The brownish fat body and black wings made him initially think it was a large moth, but the speckles of white and the slits of orange also featured in the wings resembled another creature altogether. One more familiar to him. And the moment Miles recognized the exact species of the butterfly, he was struck by a blinding flashbulb that went off inside his head like a lightning strike.

Next thing he was standing in the middle of a yard. There was a four-foot-tall chain-link perimeter fence separating the manicured lawn he was standing in and the tall, wild grass and weeds waving in the breeze of the field beyond. Within the yard was a small picnic table that he and Stephanie had dinner at the night before. Chicken salad sandwiches and slices of cantaloupe while watching the sunset. They waited outside until full dark, when the fireworks lifted off following the local double-A baseball team's end of season game. From the top of the hill overlooking the dips of the valley they had perfect seats of the display. The smell of gunpowder and the fog of smoke covering up the stars overhead drifted their way.

Aware, but only faintly, that he was experiencing some form of hallucination, Miles recognized his surroundings as Stephanie's old apartment out on Cunningham Road. A place she lived some thirteen years earlier when they first got together. At his left in the yard stood a winding willow, the branches curled underneath a canopy of wispy leaves. The leaves rippled in waves from a western breeze bringing in rainclouds. Out in the vast yard beyond stood a dilapidated barn. The old weathered beams of the structure were long past their prime, eaten away by years of decay and rot.

There was a crick in his back as he stretched. In his right hand he held a trowel. Old dirt and flecks of mulch not only clung to the toe of the blade but were also embedded between the creases of his knuckles and under his nails. He had just been removing weeds from the garden and was taking a break when the door opened behind him.

"Miles, look at this."

Coming towards him down the short steps out of the apartment was Stephanie. A much younger Stephanie. In her hands was a small aquarium with a sheet of mesh covering over the open top. "It hatched."

Within the confines of the glass, next to a deflated sac that had been partially devoured, a brown-bodied insect clung to the underside of the mesh. The wide body type, he observed, was moth-like, but the intricate design in the wings resembled that of a monarch butterfly. He'd never seen anything like it.

"I wonder what kind it is," he said.

"I was just looking it up," said Stephanie. "It's called a Painted Lady."

The creature's tiny feet felt along the ridges of the mesh, the antennae shifting like eyebrows, curious. The wings flickered movement.

"Guess it's time we let you go," said Miles, tapping a finger against the glass.

In quiet agreement, Stephanie set the aquarium down in the grass before carefully peeling back the mesh held in place by two strips of Scotch tape. The butterfly was, at first, reluctant to explore, still grasping the mesh while the entire world was now open to it. Miles gently brushed the backs of his fingers in a sweeping motion toward the insect, giving it a nudge. The Painted Lady let go and took shaky flight. The breeze helped carry it on its way.

A warm arm slipped around his back, her hand clutched his waist. Together they watched the butterfly cross over the boundary of the fence and skitter along the taller blades of grass. The clouds barged in as the gusts picked up, bringing in the scent of rain. Miles and Stephanie waited until the creature vanished beyond their sight.

Back in the driver's seat of his truck, Miles's first instinct was to stomp down hard on the brake, panic-stricken that the truck had started coasting during the daydream that stole him away. To his relief the truck hadn't moved an inch. But from behind came the long bleating of a car horn; the traffic light signaled a green arrow for the left turn. Miles held up an apologetic hand in the rearview and made the turn off the parkway.

As soon as he was able on the adjacent street, he pulled over to the curb and threw the truck into Park. Soaked in a flash sweat, Miles took a moment to collect himself, his thoughts. What the hell had just happened? His pulse raced, his hands—when removed from the steering wheel in a grip that drained the blood from his fingers—were shaking. He removed his glasses and wiped away sweat with the inside of his forearm. The worrisome part of him was convinced he'd just suffered a stroke or some other disabling attack. The vision he saw, that he experienced, had felt so real. Much like the dream from that night. Much like the ghostly touch of his wife. Surely, he believed now, these things were all related, and it triggered in his mind that something wasn't right.

Except he felt fine. Better than fine.

He felt awake. More awake than he had in a long time.

He also felt the crawling of an itch, burrowing deep inside. A gentle prodding that spoke to his muse.

Inspiration.

Not only did he *want* to draw, he knew *what* to draw.

It had been the butterfly that put things into motion. The sudden appearance of what Miles believed now to have been a Painted Lady flying over his windshield had set off the memory like a bomb waiting to go off.

But, much as he looked around, even getting out of the pickup and scanning around the intersection, there was no sign of the small creature to be found.

Time was of the utmost importance. The inspiration, he knew, wouldn't last. It never did. And when a burst came dawning upon him like it had, it was not to be wasted. With a sense of renewed purpose,

Miles hopped back into his truck and raced the two blocks to the apartment. He'd have to check his supplies, make sure he had what he needed to get started. Which meant a trip down into the basement. Where his one and only painting from the last nine months had been stowed away.

His internal voice made sure to toss in its two cents.

Now you're really losing it.

There were other things stored down in the cellar. Six large storage tubs housed things from home that Miles couldn't be without. While some of these belongings—a diary Stephanie kept, notes she left for him, photos, among other keepsakes—he couldn't bear to keep in sight, there was comfort knowing they were there with him. Just out of reach.

Visits to the cellar were not frequent. The washer and drier for his apartment were set up in the breezeway out the back door from the kitchen. Beyond making sure groundwater from the winter's thaw wasn't snaking up through the floor drains and compromising the furnace or water heater, or the six storage tubs, Miles hardly went down there at all.

He stood hesitant on the landing just inside the apartment's back entrance. The descending steps to his left dissolved into the dark. Every few seconds, from out of the blackness of the cellar, came a drip of water breaking the silence. Each drop echoing as it landed inside puddles pooled sporadically on the concrete floor. *Plink. Plink.* Groundwater from the recent string of springtime storms that had nowhere else to go. Interrupting the rhythmic dripping of water came the whirling startup of the building's sub-pump. The collected water in the basin of the pump was sucked up and then noisily shot through the pipes and deposited outside only to sink back into the already moistened soil. The running hum of the pump made the landing quiver beneath his feet. Then everything settled.

The slow dripping resumed. *Plink. Plink.*

Each breath felt different with each step he took creaking under his weight. Once he was enveloped in the dark, the air tasted different. Cooler. Dank. Five miles down the parkway there was both a Michael's Art Supply and an A.C. Moore's, but Miles wouldn't allow himself to turn back now. More so, the voice of reason wouldn't let him avoid the task of retrieving his old art supplies. Not because of some old painting he stashed in the back corner, nor the memories closed away in one of the five other remaining storage bins kept down here.

It's just a damn basement.

It's just stuff.

"This is . . ." and he made himself say it, sighing in exasperation, "silly."

At the last step before the bottom he reached out into the void and found the one dangling string among the unseen conduit of pipes, wires, and vent work. The naked lightbulb snapped on dim and slowly burned brighter, illuminating only a short spotlight that stretched a few feet beyond where he stood.

Five feet away, along the dirty and cracked floor, the basement split into two halves, separated by a stained concrete wall.

Through the doorway on the left was the half of the basement reserved for him. It was dark beyond the threshold, no windows on his side, whereas strong rays of sunlight pierced through three muck-stained windows in the foundation on the right side. Besides a separate water heater, furnace, and electrical box on the right side of the basement there were only a minimal amount of discarded items left behind by previous tenants. A dust covered card table stood folded up leaning against a far wall. Two plastic lawn chairs and a small wooden step-stool collected dust in the back right corner. Four wooden pallets were scattered about, slowly decaying from moisture. A splintered broom lay across the dirty floor.

Miles took a deep breath before entering his side of the basement. His nose wrinkled at the hanging scent of mildew.

No windows had been built into the left side of the cellar. Had there been, the view would look out at a privacy fence that ran the length of the side yard as well as the base of a towering pine. Another lone bulb hung from the ceiling, its drawstring about five steps in. Miles knew where to find the cord among the continuing lines of pipes and old wires. The light popped on with a gentle tug.

He was already looking at the bin he shouldn't have when the pale light revealed everything within mere steps of where he was under the bulb. Six bins—four of them blue, one black, and one red—were set on pallets to keep them above the often damp floor. Like the drawstring, he knew right where to find that red storage bin before chasing away the dark.

Of course, said the voice. *You just couldn't make it easy on yourself.*

The plan had been to come down and spend no more than a minute snatching the bin he needed and hauling ass up to the living room. Everything could be sorted through up there. That was the plan anyway. Until the red storage bin was in front of him.

It was too late to look away, too late to ignore. Each of the six bins had on it a label with a name. The red one's name was *Stephanie*

The black bin was the one with all the art supplies brought over from the house. It was right there, not more than a stretch beyond his reach, sharing a pallet with one of the blue bins full of other household keepsakes. He still could have grabbed the art bin and run upstairs, but instead realized he'd been kidding himself all this time. *You were always going to open it*, said the voice. No matter how much he convinced himself otherwise before coming down, the outcome was a foregone conclusion.

After what he had felt that morning—her foot entwined with his, the sleepy yet surreal touch of her skin against him—it gave Miles reason enough to believe that maybe, possibly, in some way, she wasn't entirely lost to him.

He pried up on opposite ends of the red lid. The plastic top came loose with a snap.

Stacked inside were numerous wooden boxes—eight in all—each the size and shape of a shoebox. On each of the lids were different paintings that distinguished them. They were memory boxes. He had started collecting them and filling them and applying the paintings shortly after he and Stephanie's relationship started growing deep roots that proved difficult to unearth. The earliest box was set among those on the top of the stack. The front façade of the Sunset Moon Café decorated the lid. Of the many times they frequented there over the years, Miles had saved such things as the receipt from their first order, ticket stubs from the bands and poets they'd gone to see, as well as the fully stamped Tour 'Round The World cards they earned each year for trying the revolving cast of twenty imported beers kept on tap. The remaining seven boxes all had their own themes, spanning the length of time through their wedding to the years after, ending just short of her death the previous September.

There was a box with a butterfly painted on the lid. The insect was nestled between two gerbera daisies—Stephanie's favorite flower—the bottoms of the stems coiled around each other. This was the box he made for their wedding day. The daises were painted orange and red to match the bouquet she carried that early autumn afternoon. This was the box he opened.

He sifted through a pile of Save-the-Dates, formal announcements, and drafts of invitations. At the bottom lay a blue envelope with his name written in his wife's bubbly cursive. On that crisp, overcast day when they traded vows—made colorful by the turning foliage spread over the hills—he had found this lone envelope waiting for him as he paced laps around the rectory of the church.

As he had then, Miles traced over the indentation of his name, feeling the curvy impression left by the pen in his wife's hand. The face of the card inside had a swath of fireflies forming the shape of a heart rising out of tall grass at sunset. Black text ran into the fading light of the sun dropping below the horizon. It read: *Once You & Me . . . Now Us.*

Though he knew the message inside by heart, he opened it anyway. And just like on that day, his fingers trembled. His heart rose into his throat.

There was no stock message inside the card, just the writing of his soon-to-be bride.

Miles,
  What is there left to say? Our day is finally here, finally real! No words express how I feel right now. No words, except: I DO!
  See you soon!
  Your (almost) wife (!!!),
  Steph

Taking in a drag of the cool, musty air, a clench hit the base of his throat, choking him up as he lingered on her words. A surge of warm tears crept into the corners of his eyes. His vision became momentarily blurry. Opening the card was akin to tearing off a bandage and taking the scab along with it. Strangely, though, there was an addictive quality to the pain. It was like he needed to feel it sometimes, needed to feel something. Needed to feel how much he missed her.

Now he just wanted out of the basement.

The box lid went back on, followed by the top for the red bin. Once he had the black bin with his art supplies in his arms, a tug on the draw-string returned his side of the cellar to absolute dark. On the way out he sensed what felt like eyes watching him. Eyes from the back far corner. There was nothing to see, but Miles knew it was there.

A black plastic bag. What was inside pierced the dark, sending waves of unease through Miles's guts.

He sighed, and winced at a cramp.

Probably shouldn't have had any of those chicken wings after all.

He carried the black bin upstairs, forcing himself not to look back.

After unlatching the lid, he found there was even less inside than he thought. All the supplies Miles brought from the house had been packed tight to keep the more sensitive materials—the charcoal sticks, the small tubes of acrylic paints, and the loose sheets of sketch paper—intact. Square yards of blue fleece had been rolled, some folded, and placed within and on top to pad the materials.

First thing he came across was a cinched freezer bag full of used pencils. There was a wide variety of leads stored inside; from the top brand names—Stetsons and Artisans—to the ordinary No.2 Ticonderoga pencils. The Ticonderoga brand was Miles's favorite. The leads were soft and pliable, perfect for adding the right amount of weight and shade. Perfect, as well, for smearing and smudging. Flexible enough also for soft lines. Ticonderoga graphite was simple to erase with a plain kneaded eraser without leaving remnants or streaks on the page. He preferred them when starting out.

Having drawn pictures from an early age, long before he ever put solid sentences to paper, Miles never gave too much credence to the claims of better quality from the more expensive or prestigious brands. A real artist could work with anything. The plain Ticonderoga was his weapon of choice. The first work he ever sold was at age fifteen and that was created with a number two Ticonderoga. The picture was a literal take on The Big Apple, displaying a giant piece of the fruit amidst towering glass skyscrapers and old brick towers in the middle of Manhattan. The picture hung as part of his high school's exhibit at the Anam Cara studio downtown and was bought for one hundred and seventy-five bucks. Sure, the purchase was made by his aunt Sallie, but still, it was his first, and decorated the wall proudly in her sewing room for many years.

The Ticonderoga Miles removed from the freezer bag had long been worn down to about four inches long and featured bite impressions down its yellow scrawny length. It occurred to him as he studied it that this very pencil was the one he used to sketch the face that randomly popped into his head eight months ago, right here in the living room.

The pencil had been gripped between his front teeth once he began applying paints to the drawing. He'd been so focused on the impromptu project, he hadn't realized just how tight his body had been, how constricted his muscles, until he was finished. His jaw ached, teeth sunk deep into the soft yellow wood. The bland taste of the pencil slathered on his tongue.

While he painted, the light of the day shifted to overcast. It had been warm and muggy for late fall, the windows open, the scent of old soil, dying leaves, and a cold rain on the breeze that was gathering strength. The strange and unfamiliar face that had begun haunting him was filling in with color. This was the only way he thought to get the image out of his head.

The storm blew in. Ribbons of cascading rain thrashed against the open apartment windows, permeating the screens and soaking the carpet. Miles ignored it all in favor of hope. Hope that this work would be his sobering up, banishing his demons. A sense of purpose restored, he kept at it fervently, passionate when it came to the details: the way the light fell on the curves and arcs and slopes, matching the image that was so clear, so precise in his mind to its most minute characteristic.

The late autumn storm provided a background score. His art, like the most intimate moments with Stephanie, required everything of him. His focus, his passion, his vulnerability. When it came to the picture, all of him was on display.

Where it was atypical for Miles to begin and finish a work in a single session, in this instance there couldn't be a break. There could be no leaving the sketch for a day to allow a moderate disconnect and then come back later with a more objective eye. This picture wasn't being made for scrutiny. It wasn't for anyone else to see but him. There was no time to dissect the work of all its faults and later fix them. The picture would only have him—all of him—just this one time.

He applied the right mixture of brown for the eyes, the creamy skin, infusing the right shine for the lips. Then he filled in the butterflies, the hundreds of them swarming.

When it was over, he hurt.

His neck ached from the strain, his back cried out from all the time spent leaning over the canvas. A soft indentation along the inside of his right ring finger—a pocket of flesh where all of his tools rested while working—had swelled to a sore deep purple. The hinges of his jaw were tight. On his tongue he tasted the waxy coating of the wood and lead. Goosebumps raised on his bare arms from the flow of cool wind coming in through the dripping windows. The storm had passed. Goosebumps also flared up along the rungs of his spine, but not because of the chill. He took in the finished picture.

Besides his wife, he'd never seen something so stunning, so intimately beautiful.

He cried, which wasn't uncommon anymore.

The picture was finished, the face out of his head, but after the initial moments studying the work, he found he could no longer look at it.

And so he buried it.

After scavenging the contents of the black storage bin, Miles came up with a sketchbook. Only half of the pages were occupied with drawings. There were no empty canvases. The sketchbook would do.

The yellow cover depicted a pencil touching the edge feathers on the wing of a great bird, an eagle perhaps. The word WINSTON ran along the bottom in a rigid black font.

Miles flipped through the pages, paying no mind to any of the previous entries—light practice sketches and doodles—and stopped at the first blank page about midway.

After all of this time, the Ticonderoga fit perfectly into the soft pocket of flesh on his right ring finger.

He had the blank surface of the page waiting. He had the pencil. Most important, he had an idea.

There was no excuse now, no reason to dodge when the voice said: *Why not begin.*

He propped the Winston sketchpad against a raised knee, his back up against the edge of the coffee table. In his head the image of the Painted Lady was as fleeting as the creature itself, moving off toward the horizons of his memory. He had to start quickly before the sight of it was too far gone.

Miles closed his eyes and tried to focus. Oddly, with little effort, once he was seeing with his mind in place of his eyes it became easier to envision the butterfly as it scampered off. But it wasn't the insect tracing over his windshield that was there. Instead it was the recently hatched butterfly that he and Stephanie set free so many years before; every detail captured in his imagination down to the dozens of tiny white spots embedded in its black and orange wings.

A strange calm wafted over Miles, settling his unease like an unexpected but very much welcome cool shot of air on a stifling summer afternoon. At the same time an unusual confidence rose within him. He moved his hand wielding the Ticonderoga and touched the tip of the pencil to what he knew, though couldn't see, to be the very center of the sketchbook page. His eyes remained closed as he began to move the pencil over the page.

You know this is impossible, right?

Despite knowing there was no way even the most rudimentary shapes could be done to perfection on the page without looking at it, but trusting what his instincts and not what the voice of reason was telling him,

Miles's hand followed the slopes of the butterfly's wings that he could see in his thoughts, every inch of the creature accentuated in the dark.

There was no temptation to peek. There was a concern that if he opened his eyes the image of the butterfly would leave him. So he kept his hand moving, making out the details in the wings—the slices of orange against the black compared to cracked glass. When he wanted to shade or soften the lines he brushed along the page with the side of his pinky. He never once reached for the eraser.

Over and over he experienced watching the freed butterfly following its wayward path beyond the chain-link fence, vanishing into the tall grass in the direction of the decrepit barn, wavering in the wind of the coming storm, feeling her arm slip around him, her hand grasping his waist.

He was finishing up with the picture, or so he believed with the last few details of the Painted Lady's body to be blindly included, when a crippling, violent interruption in the form of a blazing white flash cut through his vision like an exploding sun.

In the brief instance of the flash there was a face Miles had never seen before.

His eyes popped open to find himself back in the familiar surroundings of the sunlit living room of the apartment. He gasped for air as if he'd stopped breathing and his lungs were begging. A rhythmic drumming in his chest and a pulsing heat radiating out of his skin made him aware of the sweat that now lathered most of his body. A swipe across his forehead with his fingers revealed a moderate slick of perspiration had pooled there before snapping back into the present.

The face terrified him; he could still see it as it drifted away. The hollowed cheeks. The worn and leathery skin sunken tight to the bones of the skull. The dark eyes. The scar.

Like any dream, the image was gone within seconds but still left him with a cringing dread. The next time he closed his eyes there was comfort in seeing nothing but black.

After the thumping in his temples ceased and he was able to take a few breaths to ground himself back in the calm, warm surroundings of his apartment, Miles noticed the used and chomped on Ticonderoga was still in his right hand but the Winston sketchbook had toppled over onto the floor next to his right thigh. The picture of the Painted Lady lay face down.

How much you want to bet it's going to be on the level of something a four-year-old can accomplish with a pencil sticking out of his nose?

Except, for the first time that Miles could recall, the internal voice of reason was wrong. When he picked up the sketchbook and turned it over to examine the first drawing made in months, there was a cohesive drawing on the page but it wasn't of a butterfly.

"Holy shit."

The internal voice was silent.

What took up the page instead was the face of a man. Based on the thinning hair around the middle of the scalp and the amount of creases in the flesh, the age of the subject was maybe late thirties or early forties of a life definitely hard lived. Both eyes, hallowed, darkened underneath the eyebrows, stared back at Miles. The cheeks were sunken, the bones underneath beginning to show through. A beard of heavy stubble added to the face's unkempt appearance. There was also a scar. A curving trace of white that could only have been made by using the edge of the eraser began over the right eyebrow and made a sliding arc down along the inside of the nose, ending inward toward the middle of the cheek. Almost a perfect backward C.

Artistically there was much detail in the picture to admire. But there was also a substantial amount of alarm shriveling his insides. The longer he looked, incredulously, at that deranged face on the page, the more the reality of what happened, along with a sickening panic and drowning angst began to take hold.

What have I told you?

This was long past the borderline of crazy. Not one part of anything that had happened to him since he woke that morning, and even before if the dream was to be considered, was normal. There was also no denying or mistaking any of the strange things that were happening or explaining them away as something else, something more rational or usual. If there was any physical, tangible proof of mental instability it was looking at him, looking through him, via the haunted eyes of the scarred man occupying the sketchbook paper.

I've said it all along, Miles. The inner voice was filled with pride, wielding against him a chastising confidence. *What further evidence do you need?*

More than a little freaked out and frustrated beyond self-control, he tossed the yellow Winston away from him, its pages flapping until it folded up on the floor near the wall under the windowsill. There was only one thing that would help him, one solution.

He opened the medicine cabinet in the bathroom and snatched up his pills. Three of the Ambien tumbled out into his palm and he dry swallowed them in one go. Had more come out in the single tip and shake of the pill bottle there was little reason to believe he would have stopped himself and considered the safe dosage. Even so, after the hard swallow there was a horrible temptation to chase the three pills down with more but Miles found enough inner strength to twist the cap back on and return the bottle to the shelf. That exertion alone was enough.

Seventeen minutes later he was passed out on the bed.

The room was dark when his eyes blinked open. When he climbed in earlier he hadn't bothered getting under the twist of sheets; he just lay on top of the mess of a bed that remained as a result of the previous night's troubled rest. His cheek was cold and damp from the drool soaked into the mattress cover, his feet draped over the edge, shoes still on. It took a considerable effort to lift and turn his head enough to see the clock.

Miles fixed his glasses, which rested askew on his nose.

9:17 p.m.

He'd been out nearly six hours.

His stomach groaned, and loud.

Once he was steady on his feet he went to the kitchen with the purpose of making a sandwich with whatever there was to be found in the fridge. In a small drawer were a few slices of black forest ham and a full container of smoked turkey from Ottoman's Deli. There was also an unopened block of Kraft American cheese singles. A generous stack of all three fit between two slices of bread with a slab of mayo and whirling path of mustard. To go with the meal he grabbed a small bag of sour cream and onion chips and poured a tall glass of iced tea. He didn't make it out of the kitchen before downing the entire glass. One of Ambien's least worrisome side-effects was dehydration. He poured a second glass and drained a quarter of it before sitting in the recliner and flipping on the television.

He'd just taken a bite of his sandwich when there came the sound of footsteps moving over the ceiling. Miles muted the television. The footsteps went from one end of the room, stopping over his head, and back to the other, then carried off into another section of the upstairs apartment where they stopped altogether.

He waited, one cheek inflated with mashed bread, meat, and cheese. A drip of mustard hung on his bottom lip. He paused chewing, listening for the sound to come back. It didn't.

Before he unmuted the television his eyes fell upon the floor underneath the windowsill just beyond his reclined feet. The Winston sketchpad lay closed and face up, the cover drawing of the great eagle soaring in flight. He didn't want to think about it. Thankfully, his inner voice took pity and remained quiet.

He finished his dinner, finished his iced tea, and found an old war documentary on the History Channel to take his mind off everything.

Every so often he caught himself twisting the wedding band he still wore on his left hand.

He didn't want to think of anything, but some things were impossible to ignore.

After the initial lines are made and shapes begin to take up room on the page, an artist starts to realize the scope and depth of The Work.

They also realize the result will not be quite what they anticipated.

He'd never seen snow falling at the beach before. And despite any efforts by Stephanie and her parents to convince him, he stubbornly offered to remain skeptical. Said he would believe it when he saw it.

Her parents lived in the same neighborhood a mile from the ocean in the small coastal town of Old Orchard Beach, Maine, where Stephanie was raised. Miles accompanied her to the shore for the holidays. They'd been together ten months and he had yet to meet her parents. A Mainer at heart (or "Mainiac"—though only those living along the Maine coastline were allowed that term), Stephanie was defined by her straightforward manner. In their dinner table discussion on weather at the coast, she assured Miles all the same types of systems that occurred inland also happened on the beach.

"Sometimes," her father added, "what happens on the beach can be worse than here, and we're only a mile in." Hank was a gruff, tall man facing the onset of his sixties. Also the very no-nonsense type. "Summers here are one thing—not too hot, and we get storms, nothing like tornadoes very often though—but winters are typically brutal. The northeast is always good for a blizzard or three with the way these things move up the coast, getting their strength from the water."

"Well," said Miles, trying to keep all hint of ulterior motive out of his voice, "maybe we'll see some snow while we're here."

The front end of their stay at the Maine shore had been quiet. Relaxing. Clear blue skies and crisp but comfortable temperatures in the high thirties, unlike back home in Serling Oaks where the skies remained soupy gray, chills in the single-digits to lower teens, and a daily run of snow showers and surprise squalls as front after front continued forming off the Great Lakes. Miles was beginning to wonder if he would have to modify his plans any as they neared the end of their visit in Old Orchard. The chance for any snow, even a passing flurry, seemed less and less likely with each passing day as the sun rose bright and unobscured. They'd gone for walks on the boardwalk in the mornings and

Miles contemplated whether timing and the picturesque view of what he pictured in his mind as the perfect moment meant anything as long as it was with the right person. And Stephanie was the right girl. Of course it didn't make things easier walking the boardwalk overlooking a vast and sparkling Atlantic, one hand in hers with the other holding a small box stashed away in his coat pocket.

In the end he was glad he held out.

Two days before they were to make the return four-hundred-mile drive back to New York, the formation of a winter storm occurred just north of the Carolinas and started climbing up the coastline. Quickly expectations rose and wild speculation had this storm surpassing even the Great Blizzard of '93. Meteorologists on both coasts were giddy with orgasmic delight as each new forecast model offered a more reliable, and quite significant impact. They were calling this one the Storm of the Century.

It even trended on Twitter as #SNOWLOCAUST.

"As you can see here," pointed out lanky weatherman Jeremy Simms on an interactive map of the northeast, "this is really the odd mixture of two systems coming together—forced together—to follow the same track by a combination of this winding jet stream that's gone far south and pushing everything north and this stationary Low out in the Atlantic, which itself is keeping everything along the coast." Miles and Stephanie and her parents sat in the living room with a roaring fire crackling in the fireplace, watching the latest developments. The storm was less than twelve hours out. Pressing a series of buttons on the clicker in his hand, Weatherman Simms advanced the timeline of the storm to the early hours of the next day, when the spinning blot of the massive storm would climb above Manhattan, overspread Massachusetts, Connecticut, Rhode Island, and Vermont, and then move in to smother much of New Hampshire and Maine, which were predicted by forecasters to take the worst of a direct hit as the system was expected to stall. "Given the nine inches that's already fallen in New York City, we're looking at, at least, a day-long, maybe even thirty-six hour event for those of you farther north where the storm will pause and continue to grind. Cleanup will extend into the next few days for sure." Another click of the remote revealed colored bands that predicted snowfall totals once the storm began to move away from the coast.

Old Orchard was centered in a band of violet that indicated a total of eighteen to twenty-four inches of snow. More could even be anticipated as a result of blowing or drifting snow depending on sustained wind.

"Hopefully, if you're watching us from one of these soon-to-be heavily-impacted areas, wherever you are tonight . . . you have plenty of provisions, and don't mind being stuck there for a while."

As the weatherman threw it back to the main anchors, Miles fought to restrain a grin he didn't want anyone else in the room to see. Especially Stephanie. In the pocket of his jeans was that same small box he kept with him at all times during their stay. No longer was he concerned about making the perfect moment. Now he just had to take advantage of one, as the perfect moment was coming to him.

The next morning, Miles sat right up, wide-eyed, and took a gander out the guestroom window with the hope of spotting a dusting on the ground or even the first flurries beginning to fall. Throughout the night the weather app on his phone had buzzed alerts about advisories and warnings being issued for the Maine coastline. A Winter Storm Warning had been issued for the inland due to impending heavy snow. But out the window he saw that not a flake had come down. The ground was dry and the skies were white with no promise of being a threat.

It was that ethereal calm. The silence before the big yawn.

A soft knock at the door and Miles quickly stashed away the small box that had rested next to his phone and glasses on the nightstand. The handle made a slow turn, light spilling in from the hall as the door opened and Stephanie stepped inside. She closed the door gently and approached the bed. Her unruly morning hair unspooled in kinky curls framing her concerned-looking face. "Morning." Her voice was not quite awake.

He smiled at her. "Morning."

She sat down next to him on the bed. "What's up?" he asked.

"I've been thinking," she said, cautiously. "Maybe we should leave early."

It was a move he anticipated. They only planned to visit with her parents until the next day and now the storm threatened to keep them in Old Orchard until the end of the week depending on clean up and travel bans.

"It hasn't started yet," she said, "and maybe if we go and don't make any stops we can get home before it gets really bad out. If we leave in an hour we should make it back around noon." Concern then really set in. "If we get stuck here we could get snowed in for a while."

It was hard for him to argue. The smart thing would have been to leave. But leaving didn't coincide with his plans. It was being selfish, but Miles knew as much as he wanted to be back home with her in their apartment, they had to stay. The trouble would be convincing her not to pack up and go.

"We don't even have to shower," she said. "We can eat a quick breakfast with them and get on the road. We'll have plenty of time to shower later." She wasn't even trying to be subtle here. "Plus we'll be snowed in at our own place."

Her plan, especially where she mentioned showers, was near next to impossible to turn down. But he had to. He had to keep in mind the little box that was hidden under his pillow. It was a reminder of sacrifice being worth the reward.

"How's that sound?" she asked. "You ready to go home?"

He tried to lighten the mood. "You tired of your parents already?"

She responded with narrow eyes and a jab to his arm. Though they laughed and shared a deep kiss in this private moment together, it pained him to air far on the side of caution in order to keep them there. Pained him literally because staying meant a few more nights camped out alone in the guestroom on fold out mattress with the stiff springs poking through to his back.

But again he thought of sacrifice and reward.

"If we were to leave and be home before the worst of it," he said with a sigh, "we should've left yesterday."

He expected her to argue that her vehicle, a Honda CRV, was more than equipped to get them home safely, to which he was ready to respond that it wasn't her driving that worried him but that of others on the road. If necessary he would have continued on, saying that trying to get back now might mean getting stuck for hours on the interstate if they came upon gridlock due to any accidents. And there were sure to be accidents.

But she raised no opposition. Her disappointment, though, was clear.

"At least now we can see snow on the beach," he said. "How many chances do you get to go in a full-blown blizzard?"

She raised an eyebrow, suspicious. "You and this beach thing—I've told you: It snows on the beach!" She huffed. "If I thought for a second you controlled the weather I'd think you were up to something."

He said he could take no credit for their situation, but dodged her claim of having something planned. He once again pictured the small box under his pillow.

After the passing of midday and still not a trace of a flurry had come down out of the heavens, Miles began second-guessing if they should have tried leaving early. If the storm was delayed or had changed course they could get home and spend some alone time together before going back to work the next week.

While out to lunch at a diner with her parents, Miles meant to pull her aside the first chance he could get her alone and say they should follow her plan, pack up quick and leave. While in the restroom he held the small box open, staring at the silver ring tucked inside. In the haste that would ensue trying to leave, if she agreed to it, he didn't want to rush the proposal he'd so carefully planned, knowing all along that Mother Nature was the wildcard, a variable he couldn't depend on cooperating. It was a romantic scene in his head worthy of being written into a Nicholas Sparks novel: an empty beach, gray clouds circling overhead with a slice of sun shining through, the calm ocean washing in, receding, washing in, a gentle snowfall reflecting the light, he and Stephanie walking, they stop, he bends down, one hand in hers, the other holding the small box open in front of her.

Too perfect.

And, apparently, too much to ask for.

He exited the bathroom with the intent of suggesting they head home when, out of the line of windows wrapping around the diner, his eyes grew at the sight of the near whiteout of snow coming down almost sideways.

The lot was covered as they made their way to the car.

Miles felt butterflies in his stomach as Stephanie took hold of his hand to keep from slipping. In the other hand, buried deep in his coat pocket, he held tight to the box with her engagement ring.

Then, something exploded.

His eyes shot open; his body jolted awake. The explosion that pierced his sleep had come from the television. A documentary on The History Channel showed the detonation of a nuclear bomb as part of a series of secret testing in the islands of the South Pacific. While the narrator droned on about America creating the world's most destructive weapon, Miles checked the time on the cable box. It was just after one in the morning.

He was about to stand from the recliner when he noticed his right hand; his palm was up, fingers curled around something he couldn't see, but something he could feel.

It was Stephanie's grip on him, how her hand squeezed his as they crossed the snow-covered lot over a decade ago. Much like before, the feeling of her from his dream had bled into the real world. And also, same as before, her touch lasted only a few seconds before fading away. He flexed his fingers to see if the feeling would come back. It didn't. She was gone again. He sighed deeply.

When he felt able to, he pressed in the footrest of the recliner and stood. The Winston sketchpad remained where he had tossed it, on the floor under the window. The cover image of the great bird faced the ceiling. Miles didn't want to go anywhere near it. The closest he went was within reaching distance of shutting off the television.

Because you know.

In the bathroom he splashed cold water on his face. He tried ridding himself of the scarred face that was materializing in his thoughts. He could see the image from the page worming its way in even with his eyes open. The sickly, emaciated face staring at him. The curving scar. Droplets of water flying through the air with each splash against his face spread over the surface of the vanity mirror. In the glass he took note of his wrought expression.

Look at you, the voice of reason said. *Look at what you've become.*

"What the hell's wrong with me?"

He put a hand on the glass. The drops streaked over his reflection. Miles slid his hand along until catching on the edge.

Go ahead. Open it.

He did.

The bottle of Ambien sat on the far left of the middle shelf.

You know you want to.

He did.

It was a moment of pure weakness not lost on him, yet Miles couldn't stop himself. He winced at a hard swallow that ached his parched throat. He reached for the bottle. It was so easy to visualize all of the red pills being washed down with scoops of faucet water. Then he could sleep. It really would be so easy, and painless. This the voice told him as he had his fingers on the cap when there came a pattering of footsteps overhead.

His fingers slid off the cap. Miles listened as the steps traveled away. The floor above stopped creaking. The entire house slipped back into a summery silence that left only the occasional chirps of nocturnal insects in the background. Miles didn't even regard the pills again, instead closing the medicine cabinet and going back out to the living room.

He had to know who was up there.

From a toolbox behind the sofa he pulled a small flashlight. The projecting circle of light in the stairwell leading up to the second floor apartment was faint and yellowed but enough to guide him.

Before reaching the landing, he fumbled through the three spare keys on the ring to find the one marked APT2. The key hadn't worked earlier but Miles wasn't giving up so easy this time. He was on a mission. Determined. He had to know the crossing of footsteps over his ceiling wasn't just his imagination getting the better of him, that he wasn't crazy like the voice in his head had told him.

I guess you were finally owed one, eh?

As Miles took the last step, key at the ready, he panicked to thumb off the flashlight.

There was light spilling out from under the door.

He should have called the police. It would have been the smart thing to do, he knew that now, rather than investigating strange noises in the middle of the night all by himself. Once he saw the pool of light peeking out onto the landing from under the door, the tough act he adopted down in his own apartment had vanished. People that broke into unoccupied residences weren't known to be the stand-up noble type. More along the plain ol' dangerous type. Even hopped up on drugs type.

You weren't always the brightest crayon in the box.

Slipping the keys back into his pocket as quietly as possible, Miles put the small flashlight between his teeth, ready to lift one foot to slowly begin his retreat back down the stairs. He knew right where his cell phone was on the coffee table and now had every intention of dialing for assistance. Soon as his left heel was up and all the weight shifted to his right leg there was a loud creaking in the boards of the landing, and a shadow from the other side of the door cut through the stream of light.

Miles closed his eyes and whispered with a mouth full of flashlight, "Fuuuck."

Whoever was on the other side of the door remained there, waiting. To Miles complete shock when his eyes lifted off the floor, he concluded they were probably watching him through the peephole.

"Fuuuck."

Before he could react outside of the flashlight dropping loose from his jaw, the lock was snapped loose and the door flung open. A blinding light from inside bathed over Miles, causing him to throw a hand up to shade his eyes. *Jesus*, he thought, *are those four-hundred-watt LEDs?* In order to see anything he had to squint, and even then he couldn't determine much until a silhouette in the shape of a woman stepped in between the doorframe, blocking the light's most intense rays.

Of the shape, Miles could just make out the sharpened curve of a well-defined jawline. As his eyes further adjusted more of the woman settled into focus. Her soft-looking flesh, of what he could see, bared no blemishes and had a tone similar to that of caramel. She wore a simple white tee and black yoga pants that ended at her shins. Eyes that were a few shades darker than her mocha skin peered out at him under long bangs of shiny black hair swept diagonally across her forehead. She studied him.

Then, she spoke. "Yes?"

But before he could respond, Miles found that he was suddenly over-whelmed. Not only was he unable to speak—it was as if his tongue had swelled—but he was also clutching for the wall with one hand to keep his balance. The other hand went to his chest. A humming of white noise invaded his eardrums. Tiny black streaks and specks disrupted his vision. Inside his chest it was a symphony of pins and needles buzzing. A sweat broke out on his brow. He had just enough time to wonder if he was having a heart attack when it all passed.

"Are you all right?"

The voice of the woman was soothing. Calm. The radiating waves that had just worn off didn't come back. When she had spoken this time he heard her voice for how it really sounded. His ears perked at the smooth key of her register.

"Yeah . . ." he said, to his own surprise. He no longer needed to hold himself up using the doorframe. "Yeah, I think I'm okay. Just, uh, tired I guess."

He felt a lot better than he told her, he just didn't know why, and he didn't know how to explain it. No longer were his thoughts muddied. No longer did he feel that oppressive voice in his head. He didn't know how it was possible, but Miles felt new. Clear. Like something inside him had changed.

"You don't seem so sure," the woman said. "Would you like to sit down?"

He noted that the woman didn't sound overly concerned. Her voice, while beautiful and inquiring, was missing emotion and sympathy. It was like she said things as if reading lines from a script for the first time. Like she'd never spoken to another human being before.

"No, no," said Miles. "That's quite all right." He felt embarrassed, could sense his face filling with heat. Obviously he had made a mistake in regards to thinking this woman was some kind of vagrant or drug dealer stowing away in an empty apartment. And now, standing on her doorstep after one in the morning, and nearly taking a tumble down her stairs, he felt the need to explain himself. "My name is Miles. I live downstairs and—" he was shaking his head, knowing how absurd it would sound, "I've been hearing some noises up here. Wasn't sure what was going on. But it must have been you, walking around."

Her head tilted ever so slightly, measuring him. Had she never seen another person before? "Must have," she said.

An awkward silence crept in. By this point Miles was hoping to avoid a complaint being called in to the landlady.

"Miles," the woman said, though there was no follow up. He wondered if she was just saying his name to try it out.

"Yes. And you're the new tenant? Just moved in?"

Her face was mostly obscured in silhouette but he managed to catch that she blinked once. "Just."

"I apologize if I disturbed you," he said. "I just didn't know anyone was up here—"

"You thought someone had broken in." It was if she were reading directly from his mind.

"Jimmy, the . . . uh . . . the landlady's grandson . . . he hadn't mentioned anything to me or to her about someone new moving in. Plus I haven't seen or heard any moving trucks." He gestured down the flight of stairs to the front door. "The FOR RENT sign's still up."

The woman smiled faintly with one side of her mouth. "So it is. Well, I'm here."

He noted how formal, how precise her words were. That she also remained abrupt and didn't embellish further suggested she had long reached the end of their conversation.

"Well, no worries then. Sorry if I bothered you."

Before he got down two steps the woman said, "You weren't a bother. You were very brave to come up here alone. You didn't know, I could've been some crazy person with a knife."

There was no change in her expression, nor crack of wit in her voice. From Miles slipped a nervous smile.

She clarified: "It was a joke, Miles."

He nodded, playing along; of course he knew that. "Yes, yes—very funny. All right then, you have a good night."

Once his back was turned and he was descending the staircase again it dawned on him that he never got her name. Oh well, he wasn't about to stop and ask for it now. All he wanted was to be outside with the door closed behind him, escaping the awkwardness of this meeting with the unusual new tenant.

"Oh, Miles?"

He was at the bottom, his hand had just grasped the knob to pull the door shut behind him. He turned his head up to the woman, who was now on the landing.

"My name," she said, "is Ava."

Something wasn't right. He felt that wave of disorientation return moments after stepping foot back inside his own apartment. This instance was half as intense and lasted only as long as a single breath. In its wake was still the calmest, most vivid sense of clarity he could claim to have ever felt.

With the front door closed, he remained with his back pressed against it, thinking, listening. He could hear nothing upstairs. It dawned on him that the woman didn't appear disturbed, concerned, or even surprised by his sudden appearance at her door so late in the night. She didn't look tired or have even one hair out of place. She acted, he thought, like she *expected* him.

Ava, he thought, and couldn't stop thinking about her. She said her name was Ava . . .

He felt wide awake, serene. Inspired.

He was actually smiling, and it wasn't put on.

There was also a measurable guilt. It knocked at the far back of his subconscious like it didn't want him to forget, making him wonder if he deserved to ever feel good again.

It was after two in the morning when he tried lying down. Except he couldn't sleep. He just lay there, eyes trained on the ceiling, fully awake. Mind running a mile a minute. The room was warm and muggy with little relief coming from the open window. He flailed his legs to untangle himself when it got to be too warm, too constricting.

He went from his back onto his right side. Then his left. Each time he looked at the clock.

2:38

2:46

He made a mental note to get a window air conditioner.

He returned to lying on his back.

It wasn't that he couldn't get comfortable; his thoughts were too restless.

3:03

3:24

4:11

All the while not a single sound from the upstairs.

4:25

4:51

He considered taking a few Ambien. One would put him out for what little remained of the night, two would provide a nice nap. Two might also ensure he'd be out until the early afternoon. Today was his weekly appointment with Dr. Andrews. Couldn't miss that, or be late like he had been with Bryan.

Except he didn't want to take a pill; his mind didn't want to rest.

He wanted to work.

Even after the experience of blind-drawing the face (a piece he now considered and referred to as *The Scarred Man*), Miles felt that pull, that desire. It had been dampened when he took the pills earlier but now . . .

Ava.

What the hell had she done to him?

At quarter after five, as the early stretches of dawn began to creep over the hills and slip a dull purple light in through the windows, despite wanting to sleep, Miles got out of bed and rummaged through all the drawers and cabinets in the bathroom until he came up with an old bottle of NyQuil. There wasn't enough for a full dose but he hoped enough to help him nod off.

He also remembered a window fan in his closet and grabbed that.

Though his mind was fresh and ready to work, Miles was hesitant. That slab of guilt stuck with him. How the sudden appearance of a beautiful woman in his building had seemingly stirred him up and inspired him left a bad taste, a horrible feeling. Though she was long gone, he felt he was disrespecting Stephanie and everything of a life they had built together by letting this stranger into his head.

He drank the NyQuil not because he wanted a good night's rest. He just knew he couldn't dream on Ambien.

He wanted to see Stephanie. Wanted to feel her again.

Not long after beginning a new picture, an artist finds their footing, their confidence, and embraces The Work.

Doubt slips away.

Pellets of ice and sand, along with beads of rain and snow, stung where they hit against his exposed face. The brunt of this barrage made all the worse by the strengthening wind at the shore. His hair, slick from the mixture of precipitation, was plastered against the left side of his head as he looked around in awe through squinted vision.

They climbed stairs covered in over six inches of fine white powder. A layer of ice, unseen, under the snow made the ascent near impossible without use of the handrails. The blowing torrent of snow and hail and rain mixed with sand being carried off the beach was getting into their ears, their mouths with each breath, their eyes, and their clothes as they clutched to the wooden railings that were frosted over. Every few steps they stopped to brace themselves against another blast of frozen gusts coming over the boardwalk. Once they made it to the top of the stairs they stood side by side looking out at the roiling ocean as giant waves that were black as oil rose and crashed not more than a hundred yards away across a vast plane of sand and snow. Ripples of wind combed across the frozen dunes. Through the haze of all that was being carried in the wind, they could see and feel the waves tearing open. White foam dispersed, creating a mist that rained down.

"Well, would you look at that," Miles shouted over the roar of the ocean and the howl of the wind. "It does snow on the beach after all."

This was met with a look from Stephanie.

Miles reached into his left coat pocket with urgency. The little box was still there. If something happened and it fell out, he would never find it in the mess swirling around them.

The fierce, brutal winds combined with bundled nerves brought out tears in his eyes.

She squeezed his hand. "You okay?"

He nodded and then pointed down at the beach. "Let's go down there."

She kept hold of him the whole way down the short stack of snow-covered steps. The conditions had deteriorated even more; the pelting mix of sand, ice, rain, and snow began leaving small patchy welts on any exposed skin. Though she never let on, Miles had to believe there was an obviousness to what they were doing there. Only later would he learn she had hoped they weren't walking on the beach in the midst of a blizzard for no reason at all.

The sand was stiff as pavement and crunched under their boots. Each step away from the boardwalk was an effort against the elements with Miles leading the way and Stephanie clutched to his hand. He wasn't sure how far to go—a look back in the direction they came revealed they weren't the only ones wandering the Maine shoreline during the blizzard; two figures, bundled up to their necks in Nordic snow gear, stood up on the boardwalk and pointed out at the angry ocean. They each held phones in their gloved hands and started directing themselves on where to stand. They were snapping selfies.

Miles's nerves told him to keep walking. He didn't want witnesses for this. Especially ones with cameras.

A gasp for breath coated his entire mouth with the grit of sand. After six more steps he again turned to look back. The two Nordics were gone.

"Where are we going?" Stephanie cried out.

He said: "Right here."

His nerves continued to rattle but the shivering helped to conceal that. In the moment of all that was happening around them, he wasn't sure how much of his trembling was caused by the storm and how much had to do with what was coming next.

"This is kinda scary," Stephanie said looking around, eyes as wide as she could hold them.

He hesitated, taking it all in, knowing how his life was only seconds away from changing forever. "Sure is."

While Stephanie turned her head in the direction of the rampaging Atlantic, he slid his gloved fingers along the surfaces of the small box in his pocket to find its hinges. From there he opened the box.

Time slowed. The storm eased up briefly as he removed the box from his pocket and looked down. The golden insignia of the store's swooping logo on the outside of the box shined even in the dense gloom around them. He had an inkling that she knew, that she had turned away to give him time.

With a deep breath, and fresh tears pooling in his eyes, he knelt down. His right knee sank slowly into about five inches of wet snow and sand. The box was open and waiting, held out between them in his right hand. Exposed to the woman he loved and the very worst of the storm around them was a ring made of sterling silver that managed to glow in spite of the dreariness of the beach.

"Stephanie?"

Somehow she heard him over the roar of the wind.

When she faced him, he saw she had tears of her own. He fought to speak clearly as the heaviest gusts and bursts of debris continued to thrash against his exposed face.

"I love you." That was all he could manage before he got choked up. Her eyes went between him and the ring. "You're my best friend, my favorite person in the world. I want to spend—"

She didn't wait for him to finish.

She was already nodding, fighting to keep it together. "Yes," she said. She bent down and—placing both of her own gloved hands on each side of his face—pressed her trembling lips against his. He felt her laughing, felt her crying, felt her joy, and felt her excitement. Their kiss was warm enough that, for the duration, the storm couldn't touch them.

"All right," she said once their lips were free, "can we go now?"

She helped him to his feet.

"One thing first," said Miles. He pulled off his gloves and then freed the ring from the cube of white foam in the box. She followed suit and took off her left glove. Her hand trembled and quickly turned red from the cold. Miles slid the band over her third finger. A perfect fit.

"Now we can go."

She stretched out the fingers of her left hand, admiring the new view. The ring gleamed.

He followed behind as she led a path off the beach. Due to the wind and blowing sand, their previous footsteps made in the direction to where he proposed had been wiped out, made clean. Up on the boardwalk he paused long enough to turn back and find the spot about twenty yards away where he had knelt down. That spot, the little depression where his knee pressed through a snowy patch, too, had been erased.

Once they were in the car and able to hear each other without shouting he asked her, "You knew didn't you?"

"Of course," she said. "Why else would I have let you drag me out here in a freaking blizzard?" She then apologized. "Sorry, I didn't let you finish asking me."

"It's all right," he said. He found some spare napkins in the glove box and used them to wipe off his running nose and clean his glasses. He noticed that the tears she shed had been reduced to tiny flaking icicles melting away. "That's the part I'll remember forever."

His eyes opened then. He sat up in bed, his throat making a clicking noise from the sudden, desperate gasp for air.

Blinding sun pierced the blurry world, watering his eyes. The morning light shone in through the blinds, casting horizontal strips of shadow across the bed where he lay.

For as long as he could remain absorbed in the floating memories of the dream, Miles lay still. Like a fog when exposed to the light, those memories burned off eventually. The left side of his face, the side that wasn't pressed into the pillow, felt tingly and numb. Felt, as he realized it, the way every inch of his exposed skin had after being on that beach taking the brunt of the sand and frozen rain. He flexed his jaw to a prickling sensation.

When he moved his right leg there was a spot on his knee that felt damp and cold. As if he had just knelt down on that icy beachfront.

These feelings also exhausted themselves before long.

What didn't exhaust itself however, what only seemed to grow and strengthen to make itself known, drumming dully within like a second, much stronger heartbeat, was a sense that carried right along through his sleep, which, to his surprise, by the readout of the clock on his dresser, had only lasted twenty-seven minutes.

His mind was still sharp. Focused.

He still very much wanted to draw.

Miles figured if his mind and his body were telling him he was ready, if something outside of himself was trying to get his attention, there was no telling how long this drive would last. For all he could guess, this resurgence of motivation could turn out to be just as fickle as the phantom feelings he'd been waking to.

And if that were the case, he thought, then maybe he better start listening.

He forced himself to pick up the Winston sketchpad. He then scooted himself back on the floor until he was leaning comfortably against the front of the recliner, warm beams of sun touched the back of his neck and spotlighted the great bird on the cover. It took a considerable effort to begin turning pages.

When he came to *The Scarred Man* on the forty-first page, Miles made an attempt to get past his initial uneasiness and revulsion of the picture to study what was there. He had created it after all, even if he didn't know he was doing it at the time, and had no idea why it wasn't the butterfly he intended.

His eyes tracked the long scar down its winding trail along the inside of the rigid, skeletal face, beginning in the middle of the brow over the left eye and cutting a path down through the eyebrow along the inside of the nose before slinking back in a semi-circle at the bony jawline. The rest of the features, while not all pleasant, were quite ordinary: sunken, hallow cheeks, a triplicate of veins sprouting up near the temples, deep set eyes that hid a glossy, quiet rage, a patchy five o'clock shadow. Once he took the time to review the sketch for what it was and disassembled it, Miles found no link between himself and the ruined man on the page. Throughout his four decades and all the people he'd met and all the places in the world he'd traveled, Miles couldn't recall ever crossing paths with anyone of resemblance. The image had struck hot, like a bolt of lightning in his head, interrupting his vision of the Painted Lady. The only conclusion he could fathom was that *The Scarred Man* had been a symbol, a manifestation of all his wound up anxieties and fears and reluctance about getting back to work. About facing his drought of inactivity and resuming a normal life after so long. Outside of this, it was a damn fine sketch. Still gave him the willies.

He tore the page loose from the binding and let it go with a casual toss, choosing not to watch where it would float back down to the carpet or which side would land face up. He was moving on.

On the coffee table was his trusty Ticonderoga pencil from the day before. Once he had that chewed up length of yellow wood in his hand and the next page in front of him, Miles brought his knees in close with the pad resting against his legs and began searching his thoughts for a picture. In the moment he felt unstoppable.

Except he could think of nothing to draw. His mind was as blank as the page.

"All right, come on," Miles said, trying to get himself going. "You used to get paid a lot of money to do this." He licked his bottom lip, took a deep breath, let it out. "An idea, that's all. Just an idea."

Nothing.

"Relax," he said in a whisper, trying not to let frustration take over. "Just have to relax is all." He closed his eyes, took a deep breath through his nose. He listened to the slowing rhythm of his breathing, the steady cadence of his heart, his lips moving but no words escaping, finding his focus. The tip of the pencil touched down softly on the blank page and began to tap. *Tap. Tap. Tap.* In sync with the tick of a clock. *Tap. Tap. Tap.*

Tap. Tap. Tap.

It continued.

Tap. Tap. Tap.

The pencil no longer moved, but Miles still heard it.

Tap. Tap. Tap.

In the dark there came a distant hum, like the rumble of a train. The sound grew louder, shaking. Miles kept his eyes shut, focused. The tapping intensified. Faster. Hundreds of taps simultaneously. Another rumble, this time closer. The taps blended together. It no longer resembled the sound of the pencil or the tick of the clock. It sounded, to Miles, like the onset of rain.

A sharp white light exploded. It sounded as if the earth itself had cracked in half. In the aftermath of the flash, Miles was in the midst of a thrashing storm under a night sky. A deluge of torrential rain, thunder, and lightning laid waste to all that was around him. The spell lasted only a few seconds but left a searing impression at the front of his mind.

When Miles opened his eyes the vision of the storm was gone but he could still manage to hear a faint ringing in his ears of the combined wind and rumbling thunder and heavy rain crashing down. The world of the living room in the apartment, with the exception of the occasional bird, was quiet. Still.

He closed his eyes again and was immediately transported back into the middle of it. The rain coming down heavy in sheets to where he couldn't make out much of the surroundings. The road beneath his feet was filling up with water from backed-up drains. He caught glimpses of a wooden light pole, a few sagging power lines wavering when a gust pushed through, and the limbs of trees flailing next to lines of houses when the lightning flickered, but nothing too specific could be made out through the cascade.

He also didn't realize right away that, at the same time he saw all of this, his pencil started moving.

Once he felt his hand moving, he refrained from opening his eyes, allowing himself to sink deeper into the vision enveloping him. Before long he couldn't feel himself working. It was like dreaming but being aware of it. All Miles had any control over was trying to take in everything he was experiencing, anything that would help him capture the most significant details of his surroundings on the page. By the pale orange light of the streetlamp atop the wooden light pole he saw very little through the rain, but when the lightning flashed his view of the street multiplied. In the second or two when the street lit up, Miles picked one spot to focus on, whether it was a house, a driveway, topiary, mailboxes, the path of the road, and just kept it up as long as the vision would last. Soon he felt cold from the constant deluge of wind and rain, could actually smell the sweet scent in the air. It seemed the longer he remained standing under the storm, the stronger his senses became, the more this dream world came to life.

What he couldn't shake was the feeling that he recognized most of what he could see. This place wasn't just a randomly fabricated neighborhood his mind, or whatever, had conjured up for him. He knew this street. So he started following the path of the winding road. First it banked to the right, then left as it climbed a hill. By this point Miles was running. His legs didn't tire, his heart didn't complain about the sudden explosive effort, the extra weight he carried didn't slow him down. He did stop before the hill where the street bisected. He almost didn't, but a sign stood there marking the two roads. The street that went off from where he stood was called Pine. The road he had been following was Edgebrook. The flash of lightning lit up the words bright. The simultaneous rumble of thunder was his epiphany: there was no mistake; he read the street names correctly. This was the road he used to live on.

Miles broke out in a run, taking on the hill with no reservations. The rain intensified briefly, only until the bend in the road straightened out, and he got his first view of the house up on the far left.

His house.

The rain tapered off to showers. The thunder rolling overhead was muffled and distant. There was no lightning. Miles came to an abrupt stop in the middle of the street, rainwater running down both sides in the opposite direction. He stood soaking wet, cold, and in a state of shock.

Not only was his house there in this dream world, standing with every known detail down to spots where the old paint had begun to chip and a few of the roofing tiles had become worn and started to curl, but through the wraparound windows he could see from somewhere within there was a light on inside.

Miles opened his eyes. He was back in the apartment. The surroundings of the living room—the windows, fluttering blinds, television, light stand—came into view following a slow focus. He wrinkled his nose against the faint scent of rain and heat rising off newly paved road. Once he had his wits about him and felt centered back in the real world—closing his eyes and finding the vision was indeed gone—he examined what was on the page.

"Oh my God . . ."

It was impossible.

This new picture, like the one before, should have been an incoherent image. The reality of drawing with your eyes closed, even if you're a trained artist like himself, should have resulted in nothing less than compiled crisscrossing lines going every which way and scribbles that contained nary a recognizable shape. But there it was, and unlike the previous drawing, what was on the page this time was exactly what he intended: a horrifically beautiful rendering of a thunderstorm battering a small winding section of suburbia on the lower end of Edgebrook Road, complete with the wooden light pole, sagging wires, pelting downpour, and debris of leaves and snapped tree limbs. White cracks of lighting, ones that could only be made using the eraser, cut through the deep black graphite sky.

His house wasn't there, but he recognized a few of the nice homes lined up as belonging to his former neighbors.

If the picture hadn't turned out so well (and its quality was comparable to some of his personal best—designs he'd spent days on, whereas *The Storm*, as he was calling it, was started and finished within forty minutes), and if he hadn't felt such a swelling of satisfaction at the finished product, Miles would have been far more uneasy about the strange things happening to him. But he couldn't stop admiring the work.

It had made him a believer.

He was getting a second chance.

Later that morning, following breakfast and a shower, still full of pride and accomplishment, Miles scrolled through the Contact List on his phone and pressed SEND on a number he previously avoided reaching out to.

After three rings Bryan picked up.

"Miles?"

His brother-in-law agent sounded taken aback. No doubt concerned when he saw Miles's name show up on the Caller ID. "Everything all right?"

"Bryan, what's on your schedule today?"

Bryan thought out loud, said he had nothing after three. Miles's therapy session was at four.

"How about dinner?" Miles suggested. "You up for burgers at the Red Oak Diner?"

There was a pause over the line. Then, "Well, Miles, thing is . . . Molly's got this spinach chicken pasta thing she's been wanting to try out. Usually lunch dates are all I can get away with and I'm booked up today." He then asked, again, if everything was all right. "I can't remember the last time you called me."

Miles felt a hard lump of guilt slide over the back of his throat, obstructing and causing a tightening in his chest when he tried to swallow it down. What Bryan said was true: Miles was never the one reaching out. But he knew Bryan wasn't saying this as a criticism. It was all concern. Miles reassured him that everything was fine, adding: "Just some things I wanted to talk to you about."

Another pause before Bryan said: "Well, you're more than welcome to join us here, if you want."

Miles could hear the underlying reluctance in the offer. Bryan wasn't expecting him to accept the dinner invite, and could Bryan be blamed? How many times had such an offer been put out there before and Miles shot him down? They eventually became more out of politeness, and formality, rather than being genuine.

Bryan took it a step further this time, adding incentive.

"Come on over," he said. "You haven't seen the baby in a while. Molly would love to see you, too. We eat at six-thirty."

This was the part where Miles would decline, politely. Excuses were always different, but excuses was what they were.

But this time Miles surprised them both.

"I'll see you at six then."

With a few hours to kill before having to leave for his session, Miles was hoping to knock out, at the very least, a second picture. A substantial amount of the urge driving him had been satisfied, diminished by *The Storm*. But some of it still lingered. And it was growing. That second heart beating strong again. He thought best to take advantage and not waste a moment. Who knew if this drive, like a candle burning too long, down to the ends of the wick, would suddenly snuff itself out? He turned to the next page in the Winston sketchbook and sharpened his pencil.

He resumed his place on the floor of the living room, resting up against the foot of the recliner. Blank page before him, pencil at the ready, Miles closed his eyes and awaited the next white burst of light that would show him what to draw next.

By now he was figuring out how this process worked. He had to be relaxed, maintaining a steady, meditative pull and release of air in and out of his body. He had to search inward, drawing in, focusing on the black that dominated his sight. He was comfortable, ready, at ease, and inspired. Waiting. No ideas were coming. Miles was resolved though— allowing nothing in the realm of frustration or impatience to break his concentration.

Except he wasn't counting on the arrival of the mailman loudly stomping up the front steps and depositing a bundle of letters into the creaky old mailbox on the porch.

Miles sighed, his focus broken, and went out, pen and pad at his side, to gather the mail. Nothing but bills and junk credit card offers.

But he did a double-take on his way back inside.

Two butterflies engaged with each other, hovered over the bushes next to the front porch steps. There was the next idea.

The butterfly. Miles wondered if he could sketch one now. His first attempt had somehow altered itself midway through, the vision manipulating his mind and hand modified, resulting in the anguished portrait of the scarred man.

The uncertainty of what would transpire, while knocking on the back of his mind in the form of dread, was also very intriguing. It helped that he was embracing the uniqueness of what was affecting him. The worst was behind him with *The Scarred Man*, all his doubts and anxieties. Since then he felt pretty damn good. Why not continue?

He sat down, right there on the floor of the porch. In his hands was everything he needed. Keeping the butterflies in sight, he touched the pencil to the blank page. When the insects moved off, Miles finally closed his eyes.

It wasn't long before a blinding, numbing strike of white light stole him away. Once it faded, the visual of a butterfly—a Painted Lady—possessed him.

The winged creature—newly hatched from a cocoon it had devoured half of—beat its wings in the direction of high weeds and tall blades of grass swaying on the other side of the fence line. Miles stood in the backyard, watching the butterfly sail away on the tides of the wind underneath a gloomy sky. Stephanie was at his side. He didn't turn his head to see her, but knew she was there.

As it had been, the Miles outside of the vision, sitting on the porch with the sketchpad in his lap, eyes closed, wasn't aware of his pencil moving. When a wayward fly landed on the end of his nose then circled around and touched down on his forehead, he never flinched. Not aware at all of the fly's presence.

Only when he felt the warmth of Stephanie's arm slip around his back, her hand on his side, his arm wrapping around her, did his eyes open.

The transition back into the real world was just as jarring as the previous times Miles woke from his trance. Sweat ran over the creases in his brow, slid down his throat, and was soaking through the back of his shirt. His throat and lips were dry. Dizziness arose from blurred vision that slowly drifted. Once he felt settled back in place on the floor of the porch he observed the latest sketch, his state of awe had not diminished with this, the third drawing.

The Painted Lady, down to every detail, took up the middle of the page and was realized in such a realistic way it almost seemed to live right there on the page, ready to take flight at any moment. Miles almost expected to see the wings flex, and may not have been surprised if they had.

A nervous little snicker escaped, a mix of relief and a sudden confirmation that he was, indeed, on a roll. For having not sketched even the crudest of doodles on a piece of scrap in over eight months—the most he had used even the most rudimentary of writing utensils for was signing away his rent checks—this was a vast improvement.

The Garland Gallery, however, wasn't the place to display all your work on eight-by-eleven heavyweight sketchpad paper. Even in nice frames, sketch paper was viewed as amateur (though how many amateurs can say they've been paid to paint Harrison Ford, Tom Hanks, and Christian Bale as action heroes? How many amateurs have had work displayed down the length of skyscrapers in New York City, or hung outside of Grauman's Chinese Theatre, or hung in rows in the subway for passersby to put their chewed gum on?). He had two pictures of the eight he needed (he wasn't sure how he felt about *The Scarred Man* yet, but would include it if he found himself in a pinch, but for now *The Storm* and *The Painted Lady* would be welcome additions to his exhibition), but the remaining pictures needed to be on canvases. Miles decided he would go shopping on the way to his appointment. He was thinking of making a quick stop before Bryan's anyway.

If there was one fortunate aspect to being a world famous movie poster artist, it was that while people recognized his work hanging at the theater there weren't many who would be able to pick him out of a police lineup. Of the one or two websites dedicated to his work, not one had even a thumbnail profile shot let alone a suitable bio. How many times had he sat in the middle of a busy diner not even attracting a single eye? How many poster collectors and sellers put his work up on eBay and misspelled his last name as Green? He was, essentially, a ghost.

When he ventured into Michael's Art Supply before his appointment with Dr. Andrews, the young woman in the red work vest wearing a badge with her name (Anita) hadn't so much as furrowed her brow trying to place him while she rung out the armload of twelve-by-twenty-four stretched canvases. She didn't know who he was, and it looked like she couldn't care less. She also didn't seem to care if he carried the store's discount rewards card because she didn't bother to ask before totaling up his purchase.

"Ninety-eight forty." She had already started packing his canvases into large shopping bags, paying no mind to the crisp hundred dollar bill he extended toward her.

For kicks he mentioned: "I'm an artist."

She collected the hundred and made change, snapping off a bubble with the gum in her mouth. "So is everyone else here."

After packing the bags in the backseat, the dashboard clock showed he had ten minutes to get to his appointment.

Unfortunately there was no anonymity where he was going. His therapist knew everything.

Unlike the waiting room, there were no fluorescent bulbs in the ceiling, no standing floor lamps in the corner, no electric lights of any kind once in the office. The two-story room was lit by daylight coming in the large floor-to-ceiling windows running along the back wall. Doctor Havish Andrews (MD), a short, elderly man of Asian descent, with a salt and pepper comb-over and a thick black mustache, opened his door with a warm smile and invited Miles to come in and have a seat.

The office was spacious. Once the old Hillstrom Library, the large, drafty room contained a mix of the original art deco design along with Havish's modern furnishings. The bookshelves built into the east wall on the bottom floor and all four walls on the balcony of the second floor were full of medical encyclopedias, journals, and dissertations. The desk on the first floor, made of black metal with a cloudy glass top, was tucked back by the windows. Only a black file organizer and closed laptop were kept out. Along the west wall, hung in rows of invisible glass frames to give the illusion of floating were all of the good doctor's awards and certificates.

The floor was the original hardwood, restored and stained dark. Their footsteps toward the center of the room where two black leather chairs waited, separated by a glass coffee table, echoed off the arch ceiling where there hung a solitary non-working fan. When taking his seat, Miles noted that the glass coffee table between them contained not a single water ring, smudge, or fingerprint on the surface.

The sterile atmosphere of the office was oddly comforting. Everything clean and organized. It was also a tad intimidating. Miles could see how it might deter patients from sticking around after their session ended.

"So, how're things, Miles?" Doctor Andrews wiped clean the lenses of his black horn-rimmed glasses, crossing his legs—the cuff of his slacks riding up to reveal tan colored socks. He readied the pen in his hands after opening the binder labeled for their sessions. A man with an unusual style in wardrobe, today Andrews was in a yellow and gray flannel print button up with a solid red tie. He returned his glasses to his face, a wide, rugged face that matched the texture of the leather seats.

Miles crossed his own legs and shrugged. "I guess things are all right."

"Yeah?" In the quiet rasp of what remained of his accent, Andrews sounded pleasantly surprised. He cleared his throat while perusing notes from the previous week's session. "That's good to hear." He finished reading, flipped to a fresh page of loose leaf, and lifted his eyes.

Here was the beginning of their dance. Same steps since they began seeing each other. Andrews always began sessions with the soft taps—a round of easy feeler questions. Miles reciprocated by taking lead but not having much to say most of the time. By the close of their hour together Andrews would take over again, then it was time up and the check could be left with the receptionist on the way out. Oh, and see you next week!

Today, though, turned out to be a little different. A few new steps added in. Miles found he actually wanted to share the good news, if not only because it would shake things up a bit and not feel like he was just throwing money away.

"So I found out I have a gallery show next Friday."

Andrews cocked his head to the left, like a dog unsure of the sound he just heard. "Oh, *really?*" he said in his soothing rasp. "That's very exciting, Miles. Very exciting." Notes scribbled down. "And where will this gallery show of yours be held?"

"Local. Downtown at the Garland Gallery."

"Excellent." This one word was dragged out as Andrews jotted down more notes, a pleased grin lifted one side of his creased face. In a volume just a hair above a whisper he added: "Very excellent indeed . . ." He finished his note. "And this show, is it going to be old work? New work?"

"All new. I hope."

Andrews scribbled that down and then looked at Miles with admiration, spreading his hands palm side up as if he had no other way of expressing how immensely pleasing this was to hear. "Wonderful." Though Miles supposed it was part of the good doctor's job to feign even the slightest bit of interest in the hobbies of his patients, there was no panging of his bullshit meter when it came to the doctor's intrigue and satisfaction.

"It's been a long time since you mentioned any projects," said Andrews, "I take it things are getting better?"

"Yeah, I guess things have . . . changed, a little." Miles tried to disguise the immense pride swelling inside him, worried of the consequences of boasting. What hath been giveth can easily be taketh away. He would know.

"Let me see what's on the calendar at home," said Andrews. "If there's nothing, the wife and I would love to come out and support you at the show."

"Oh, well, that's very kind of you."

The doctor smiled and then started flipping back through his notes. Andrews stopped on a single page that featured numerous boxes where he recorded prescriptions. "Now, let's see . . ." he said with a reflective sigh. "How have you been sleeping, Miles? I see I prescribed you some Ambien a while back for . . . troubled sleep. We didn't discuss this the last few times. Do you find that the pills are helping?"

There was a lot for Miles to weigh before answering the question. Certainly he had his list of concerns when it came to the pills. Sure, they helped him sleep, helped . . . soften the rougher moments. They dimmed the bright lights of his imagination, stifling his dreams. As a result they stole away those phantom feelings—Stephanie's touch. The last connection he had to her.

Sometimes he needed that touch, and sometimes they did more harm than good.

Speaking any of this ran the risk of alarming his therapist. Andrews believed they had made a lot of progress together, distance gained over the worst of it. As it was, Miles felt his push and pull struggle with the Ambien was finally coming under control, so he gave a very generic response.

"I can say I don't have to worry about anything after I pop a few of those."

"That's good," said Andrews, who then asked about side effects, eyeing a list of checkboxes on an attached sheet for the prescription. "Have you noticed any skin rash? Short-term headaches? A racing pulse? Watery stools?"

"No watery stools here, doc."

More notes in the file. "Now the underlying purpose of the pills was to help with what you said were . . ." Andrews turned a page back to the session before the prescription was written, looking for the exact quote. "Ah, here it is. You claimed early on that you were . . . seeing things." He looked to Miles for clarification. "You remember?"

Miles nodded.

"Have you noticed a . . . lesser frequency of this, Miles?"

Certainly Andrews didn't know Miles was only taking the pills on an as-needed basis, not as they were prescribed (two right before bed, two after breakfast). Andrews's primary concern was his patient's well-being, and that meant numbing his overactive imagination during the day and undisturbed sleep every night, waking fully rested, and not feeling the figment touch of his late wife. Miles, however, couldn't bring himself to do it.

So he lied. "Can't remember the last time I saw anything I wasn't supposed to."

Andrews closed his file on Miles Greene and laid it down on the glass table between them. He re-crossed his legs and took a breath, one that sounded—to Miles anyway—full of relief. There was a flicker of a grin that stretched the mustache under the doctor's nose. "I have to say, Miles, all of this has been great to hear, and I've noticed something."

The words came with a weight that caused Miles to readjust in his own seat, his left eyebrow slightly cocking in concern of what was coming next.

"I've been worried about you for a while," Andrews said. "Seemed to be the same things every week since . . . well, the beginning. But I've noticed something this time." Andrews then gestured a hand in Miles's direction. "You've changed."

"Yeah?" Miles said. "How so?"

"You know, you're about the age my youngest daughter would have been if she were still alive. I ever tell you about her?"

In all their sessions, in all their hours together in this office where all of their conversations took place, there was little about Doctor Havish Andrews that Miles could claim he really knew. Nothing personal anyway besides his wife's affection for plug-in scents and porcelain kitten statues.

"Her name was Ellie. She ran with a rough crowd in her younger years. Drugs of all kinds for a while. Spent some nights in a lockup. Learned her lessons the hard way. But there was never a time her mother and I stopped believing she would find her way."

Andrews paused. The affinity in his voice lowered a few notches. "When she turned thirty-eight, it was like she finally saw herself in a mirror, and she didn't like what she was looking at. Or, should I say, what was looking back at *her*. Ellie rethought her life, went back to school. She took a job as a waitress because she refused my wife and I paying even one dollar towards her education. I was never more proud."

Miles caught the tiniest quiver in the old man's deflated jowls. A tremble.

"One night, she had just gotten off a double shift at the Red Oak. She took the double so she could have the next day off to take a final. Well, it snowed that evening. Two miles before she got home she came upon a car off the side of the road, lights flashing, stuck in a ditch. Her own car barely managed to stop.

"There was a man with his young daughter inside that other car. They were waiting for help, but Ellie didn't know that. She stopped to check on them."

A long pause before: "A pickup truck was coming toward the intersection from the same direction as Ellie. The light went yellow and the driver slammed his brakes to avoid running the light. The truck slid sideways, the backend clipping Ellie and the back tires went over her after she fell."

Another pause—one that stole every decibel of sound from the large room. Andrews used his thumb to swipe away a fresh tear before it fell out of his left eye.

"The man in the truck tried to keep her awake until the ambulance arrived. But once her eyes closed . . ."

For a while they sat there, neither saying anything. The groans and creaks of the old building around them filled the empty space. Every breath felt tight in Miles's chest. He felt an enormous grief for his therapist. He had no idea the man who had been helping him through such an awful death all these months had been through one of his own. When Andrews swallowed hard, the small lump covered by the loose flesh of his throat shifted.

"That was twenty-one years ago. I still remember the phone ringing; the officer who got there first, calling to tell us our daughter had died while trying to help a father and daughter."

Witnessing the release of this pain from Andrews, Miles could relate in ways not many could. He attributed loss to an old scar, making itself known at times by aching or itching. An old scar never completely heals and never lets you forget.

"She could've not stopped. So many never do. She just never wanted to be that person. My daughter wanted to be more than she used to be."

"I'm sorry," Miles said. It was all he could say. It was what he heard from others that proved the least annoying. So many times people—meaning well, of course—had said things to him that he just didn't want to hear, like *Things will get better* (They do, but they don't) and *I know how you feel* (Not quite).

After a beat, Dr. Andrews took in a breath, letting it out fast, regrouping himself, as if to say it was all behind him now, which it so obviously wasn't. "When I first met you, Miles, and learned what happened to your wife . . . I was worried. Worried you'd end up like me. I've been doing this for forty years, helped numerous people in all types of situations. But I couldn't help myself. Didn't know how to. But eventually I found a bearable peace. And after I did, a bearable happiness followed." Andrews smiled a weak smile, but it was genuine. This peace and happiness he spoke of certainly wasn't without its share of pitfalls along the way.

"So, what's different?" asked Andrews. "In a week you've made progress unlike anything I've seen in you in the last eight months. You look different, sound different. You walked in here differently. It's like the weight wasn't pressing you down. You say you have a show, so you're drawing again. It's like you woke up."

Woke up. That was funny. Miles liked that.

Woke up.

"So, Miles, what's different?"

By "what's different" Miles knew he was being asked *What's your secret?* as in *How'd you do it?* Andrews was nearing his late seventies and had just shone a light on a dark corner from a past he still struggled with, a terrible weight he continued to carry—even twenty years later. So what was the miracle cure?

Miles felt far from cured, but certainly different, better than he felt in a long time. There was the sudden, and quite welcome return of his artistic libido. But the changes started before that. A few mornings ago he had a dream, felt the first touch of his late wife. Hours later came the first flash of the Painted Lady in his head. Later there was the silencing of his internal voice that for so long undermined him, even when it was right.

The sequence of these changes traced back to that first morning, two days ago, when he awoke to the sounds of footsteps above his head. Someone in the upstairs apartment.

It's like you woke up, Andrews had said. How true. He woke up different that day.

It all went back to the arrival of the woman upstairs. How she made him feel when he first saw her, first heard her speak in the stairwell. The effect she had on him. That dizzying pins and needles feeling. How his desires and urges to draw again had stemmed from their meeting.

It all started with her.

Ava.

Once the early sketch of *The Work* is complete, an artist will examine what they have, and allow themselves distance.

Time away from the picture is essential so that an artist will grow detached. The challenge is not to return too soon so that, upon returning to *The Work*, they will see its flaws with an unbiased and critical eye.

Before he arrived for dinner, Miles made a quick stop. Carrying a small pink-and-gray-checkered gift bag, he strolled up to the Kesslers' front stoop, along the way stopping to indulge in the scent of barbeque and the sounds of happy shouting holding in the air. A large family down the block—a mother, father, and three kids—were playing horseshoes in their front yard, while a toddler bounced in a jumper nearby. Miles regarded them with a half-smile and a small tinge of envy. He pressed onto the front door, which opened before the tones of the doorbell faded into silence.

"Hello, Miles."

The striking hazel eyes of Molly Kessler widened in warm, welcome surprise. They even appeared to brighten in his presence. Perhaps a trick of the light, he thought, the sun low in the sky behind him.

One hand firm in his pocket, the other clenching tight to the string handles of the gift bag, Miles shuffled a brown shoe over the impeccably clean welcome mat and bowed his head to hide his blush.

"Hey Molly," he said. Words were hard to come by. Though he wanted to be there, and it took some convincing of himself to make it to the front door, he couldn't help the unsteadiness prickling his nerves.

"I'm so glad you decided to come." Molly stepped aside, the door opening wider. "Come on in."

Of all the minor details to take notice of—and take comfort in before crossing the threshold inside—Miles dwelled on the spotlessness of the welcome mat under his feet. Not a single blade of cut grass, not a clump of loose dirt or dried mud, nor a splice of tail from a tree pod was wedged between the fibers. Molly, always the perpetual neat freak, was still the same. She hadn't been changed at all by the continual messiness of having two children and Bryan.

By her warm reception to him, his spiking nerves were set at ease. There had been second thoughts creeping up a few blocks away before he pulled up to park at the curb. Doubts that maybe he wasn't ready for all of this yet, doubts that continued to hound him on his way to the front door when he noticed the family down the street occupied with their game of horseshoe. Molly didn't know that he nearly didn't press the switch for the doorbell because there was so much to answer for. A nauseating discomfort in having to explain what he'd been up to since Stephanie's funeral when he vanished from the family. He wasn't prepared to explain why he hadn't attended get-togethers or either of his nieces' birthdays, why he had chosen to be absent from their lives. Even though he owed them that explanation.

But in the depths of Molly Kessler's eyes—those lit up eyes that addressed him adoringly rather than questioningly—Miles saw that, far as she was concerned, he was getting a reprieve from all that.

Had his eldest niece, Myra, been home and not away at cheerleading camp, he wouldn't have been so fortunate. The chances of flapping his arms and getting an inch off the ground was more likely than escaping her curiosity unscathed. Having no children of his own to learn these lessons from, Miles observed Myra as she grew up. He learned children know no boundaries when it comes to their honesty. They only know the truth of what's in front of them. And if they want to know something they ask. He could just imagine all of Myra's questions and comments if she were around.

Uncle Miles, where've you been? Why weren't you at Thanksgiving? Or Christmas?? Or my birthday???

Wow, Uncle Miles, you got fat.

What's with the beard? Are you a hobo?

Did you lose more hair?

Then there also was the far more uncomfortable: *Is Aunt Stephanie in heaven?*

But tonight there would be none of that. Unless Lily was already talking.

Molly closed the door behind him. "I just put the water on to boil.

Hope you like oil and garlic spaghetti and lemon chicken with spinach."

He patted the small mound of his belly with his free hand. "Are you kidding? I love it!"

He did not.

In the small, tiled foyer that made up the dividing landing of the split-level home, Miles slipped off his loafers, setting them next to the other pairs of shoes and sneakers lined up in a tidy row outside the wide open closet. He followed Molly up the short steps into the living room. She paused.

"Bryan's down with Lily in her ro—" She stopped herself. "You haven't seen the baby's room since we finished it have you?"

He shook his head. Last time he had been over was with Stephanie shortly after Lily was born. By then Bryan only managed a few splashes of yellow paint on the walls and the crib built. Lily had come two weeks early. While Molly would've preferred the room finished long before (her obsessive-compulsiveness in full swing at the height of her pregnancy), the project remained at the mercy of Bryan's hectic schedule.

"You can go down and say hi while I get dinner ready. Glad you came, Miles." Molly touched him gently on the shoulder and then went off in the direction of the kitchen.

Both walls lining the way down to Lily's room at the end served as a photographic timeline to the life and times of the Kessler clan. Not a single work of art or wall sconce or clock hung for display. Instead there were copious amounts of wedding pictures, family vacation candids, and baby pictures especially. The frames were mismatched—different colors and textures—clashing with each other and the coat of tan paint on the walls. Having something of an eye for art, at least where complementary colors were concerned, Miles felt he couldn't breathe in their hallway.

The door to Lily's room at the end was partially open. Before he got there, Miles stopped to study a collage featuring the newest Kessler, taking in how much she'd grown since he last saw her. There was a snapshot in the collage near the center that was Myra holding Lily's hand, helping the baby to walk through a minefield of toys and scattered clothes. The picture looked recent. While Miles was sure the mess of the living room in the photo was enough to spike Molly's OCD, the image alone of the two girls looking at each other mid-stroll was enough to soften any heart. Or anxiety disorder.

It was an image Miles wished could've been a reality in his own home.

Adorning the outside of the door at the end of the hall that once led into Bryan's office (now relocated to the basement) were colorful foam letters spelling out LILY. This labeling of the door was something Bryan had been adamantly against ever doing again following the disaster it became trying to remove MYRA from their eldest daughter's door when she had gotten old enough to declare the bubble letters as "too babyish." Attempts to gently remove the name using a hairdryer and needle-nose pliers and then gently scraping at the backs of the letters with a flathead couldn't keep Bryan from also removing some of the paint and carving a few claw-like scratches into the wood. This resulted in Myra learning her first four-letter word.

Bryan also swore never to go through that again.

But there were the letters L-I-L-Y.

"Hello?" Miles gave the door a gentle push, watching it pivot open to a scene of Bryan standing behind his youngest daughter. Bryan was bent slightly at the waist, holding her tiny hands in his. The child was standing upright and, at just over twelve months old, maintained a steady balance on her two feet. She remained so though had reservations clear on her round face as he let go.

It tugged on every heartstring to watch this toddler realize that her tether, her lifeline, was out of reach. The flaring of her large eyes and parting of her lips questioned why her father would ever think to let her go. To witness this separation touched something deep within Miles that he fully understood, even though fatherhood eluded him. A lump built in his throat and sank with a heavy gulp.

He spoke again, in a quiet, high voice. "Heyyy there."

Lily spun her head in his direction. Her feet never lifted off the plush carpet. She wavered a little, her arms jutting out to the sides for balance. Her little face expressed a long uncertainty, likely about both her ability to remain standing and about the man she didn't quite recognize standing in her doorway.

"Hey Miles," Bryan said in a hushed voice. "We're just working on a little walking."

After a quick scan of the finished room, admiring Bryan's handiwork—yellow walls with a pink floral wallpaper sash running across the middle of the room as a border all the way around—Miles settled his attention on Lily, admiring the tiny beauty. Her eyes remained locked on him, waiting to see what he would do next.

"That's your Uncle Miles," said Bryan, pointing with a stubby finger.

Lily looked from her father back to Miles. Still hesitant. Seeing him now after they hadn't seen each other for the better part of a year was like hitting the restart button. She hadn't burst into tears yet so Miles figured he had that going in his favor.

"Go on," Bryan said. "Go see your Uncle Miles."

Despite this gentle urging, Lily remained steadfast. Her look of reluctance not faltering.

"Probably doesn't want to fall," said Miles.

Bryan waved this off. "Nonsense. She's been walking and falling for over a week now. She's used to it. Just call her over."

Kneeling down on the plush carpet, Miles softly clapped his hands together. "C'mon Lily."

Bryan frowned. "She's not a dog, Miles."

Miles passed his brother-in-law a dirty look that spoke all the words he wanted to say but wasn't comfortable letting the child hear. He held out his hands toward his niece.

"You may not remember me," he said. Lily continued to watch him, almost fascinated, her guard letting down. "I was there the day you were born. You were asleep in this little bed the nurses put you in when I got there, right up next to where your momma slept. You were so tiny. Just six pounds. Your father picked you up thinking it would wake you enough to see me. But you just nuzzled in the blanket, your eyes still closed. He handed you over. I was the first person besides your mom and dad to hold you. I remember that."

Lily seemed to forget that her father was in the room, her attention remaining fixed on her uncle. She was far more interested in him now.

The checkered gift bag Miles brought in was set down on the carpet right behind where he knelt. She watched him grab it and reach inside.

"I heard you have a thing for Minnie Mouse."

Bryan laughed. "Yeah, you could say that. She's only got about twenty of them in her closet."

From the bag Miles pulled out an eight-inch-tall Minnie plush, complete with pink polka-dot dress and iconic bow. "Well," he said. "I guess this makes twenty-one." The instant recognition on Lily's face said it didn't matter that there were twenty other Minnies in her closet; she wanted this one, too.

If there had been any fear of toppling to the floor or any apprehension of the bearded man in her room it didn't show as Lily reached out for her beloved stuffed Minnie with both hands. A big grin on her face revealed spotty areas where teeth started pushing through. She took one step in Miles's direction. Once the first step was made and she was still on her feet she raced over to accept her gift.

"Congrats, Miles," Bryan said. "You just bought the acceptance of a child. Hope you feel good about it."

Miles took the opportunity, while Lily was so absorbed with her new Minnie, to scoop both up in his arms and stand. Lily didn't resist, cry out, or really even seem to notice. He swept wisps of her black hair away from her face, basking in the liveliness and awareness of the child's large eyes as she squeezed Minnie's cheeks and chomped down on her snout.

"Can you say my name?" he asked. "Can you say 'Un-cle Mi-les'?"

In return, and at a much lower volume, Lily let out a string of sounds. "Uh-cah-ma." She was still glued to Minnie.

"Forget it man," Bryan said. "You're chopped liver; she's got Minnie now; she's gone to the dark side." He jutted a thumb toward the closed closet door. "That's why the rest of 'em are in there; when Minnie's around, none of us exist."

Her father came over and gently caressed his daughter's cheek. She was now tugging on Minnie's little black nose with her gums, wiggling her head back and forth, humming happily. "It's not true, you know."

Miles met Bryan's eyes. "What's that?"

"They say there's no such thing as love at first sight. Well, let me tell you, anyone who believes that has never had a child."

Miles pondered the truth of this. "We could never have one but I believe you."

"You guys never considered adopting?"

Lily squeaked with joy, her hands investigating Minnie's bow. Her uncle kissed her forehead.

"We talked about it," he said. "For a long time. It was just tough for me getting past the point that it was me who had the problem. I obsessed over it. Steph never blamed me. But then I guess I did enough of that for the both of us." He sighed.

"We both wanted to adopt. It was just me . . . I just couldn't get over the fact that I was . . . *broken*, you know?

With a sympathetic frown, Bryan nodded. "I know it's of little consolation, but you can watch this little one anytime." Lily was now using Minnie's left ear as a teether, oblivious that she was being spoken of.

Miles thanked his brother-in-law. "I'll take it."

Bryan leaned in and kissed Lily's temple. "You can spend a little time with her now if you want; I have a half-finished dessert in the fridge I need to work on." His voice then took on that annoying goo-goo pitch that overcomes most grown men when they talk to a very young child. *"A dessert Mommy may not be okay with because it's filled with what she would call 'unnecessary calories'."*

"Sure," Miles said. "I'll stay in here with her." But, of course, it's never as easy as that. There's always the list of instructions. Bryan gave the quick rundown of solutions if Lily became fussy (put her down), if she became whiny (sing to her or play music), if she was content (let her be).

"It'll be fine," said Miles. "Go!"

Bryan stopped himself before he was all the way out of the room.

"If she cries don't be alarmed. She does that sometimes if we're out of sight. If *you* cry . . . we're right down the hall."

Before Miles could toss Bryan the bird, he was gone. Probably better that the one-year-old in his arms didn't catch him flipping the middle finger. No telling how perceptive she was. No doubt her mother wouldn't be impressed. When the eldest, Myra, had dropped her fork on the floor while eating dinner one night and exclaimed "Shit!" Molly was not happy. She later morphed into Beast Mode when Myra confessed she heard the word from her father when Bryan tried to peel the babyish letters of her name off her bedroom door. Miles didn't need that kind of heat.

Alone with the child, he sat down in the corner rocking chair, Lilly and Minnie in his lap. All the while she remained fascinated by her cuddly Disney friend.

"I'll bet that's the best twenty bucks I ever spent."

He watched her play, observed how she breathed so quietly; puffs of air whistled in and out of her flaring nostrils. Lily studied Minnie's face with deep concentration. Her eyes didn't blink once. Her little mouth hung open in captivated wonder.

"I'm sorry I haven't been around," he said. "I'd really like to change that. Is that okay with you?"

Lily scrunched her brow. She stopped staring at Minnie and looked to him like she understood. Then her expression hardened. The color in her cheeks bloomed a rosy red—all those little capillaries pushing to the surface. Her lips pressed together, fists clenched. She grunted.

"What's the matter?" he asked.

Her eyes glossed over. Her little body tightened in his arms, feet pressing against his lap. She stopped breathing. Her face darkened to purple. There had been nothing on the stuffed animal that could've come loose for her to choke on. Regardless, Miles became alarmed.

"Uh . . . Bryan?"

Before he stood up with her to race out of the room, Lily suddenly relaxed with an audible gasp. The deep color in her cheeks instantly faded. She began breathing normal again, like nothing ever happened.

For Miles, his heart was still thundering, threatening to burst right out of his chest.

"What was *that* about?"

Lily couldn't speak but the answer came a moment later. His nose wrinkled at a foulness that nearly made him gag.

"Did you poop?"

Lily attempted to echo him. "Pup."

Now he felt like crying.

The oil and garlic pasta served with baked lemon chicken and spinach leaves wasn't nearly as grotesque as he prepared himself for. It was pleasantly quite tolerable. The long strings of greasy noodles slid their way down his gullet chased by plenty of hunks of Italian bread smeared with butter. Of course it had to be the healthier "not butter."

After indulging in molten no-bake brownies for dessert, Bryan, with a small cooler filled with ice and bottles of Sam Adams, led Miles out to a pair of Adirondack chairs on the elevated back porch. The last vestiges of the sun began slipping behind the tops of the tall oaks and maples that made up the forest. The tree line stood just beyond their enclosed backyard twelve feet below.

The dinner atmosphere had been pleasant enough. Conversation was kept light and cheery. At one point Molly expressed her excitement in going to see Miles's art exhibition. Miles remained modest about discussing the finer points of his display (mostly due to his being at a loss of knowing what all the displays would be).

He also didn't want to concern his agent. Currently Miles had in his arsenal *The Storm* and *The Painted Lady* (with *The Scarred Man* on deck as a pinch hitter if needed). The exhibition was a week away and Bryan didn't need to know he was still short on filling up space on the Garland Gallery's brick walls. Hopefully he wouldn't ask now that they were alone.

Molly had hoped to see pieces that resembled works a bit different than what he was known for.

"I hope what you're doing is stuff like the painting you gave us when we got this house," she said. "It's so beautiful. We still have it hanging in the bedroom."

Through the years Molly praised his poster designs (the Kesslers kept a collection of them in airtight tubes down in the basement), but she, and Stephanie for that matter, always said they felt a closer connection to his less commercial works, his personal paintings that he made for himself or gifted to others. What Stephanie dubbed as The Quiet Ones.

The painting Molly had spoken so fondly of was made using acrylics and depicted the scene of an old iron yard swing sitting desolate in an overgrown lawn. Titled A Summer Lost the inspiration of the slowly-deteriorating swing being consumed in the unkempt yard came from the day Miles moved his father into an assisted care living facility. The house Miles had grown up in on the eastside of Serling Oaks, 217 Romelle

Street, sat vacant after his father had been transported out, unable to take care of himself any longer due to his worsening Alzheimer's, and placed into the care of the staff at Woodland Park. The last one to leave the old property that day, Miles lingered, taking in the neglected backyard with fondness—many memories of pickup football games, playing catch, barbeques came flooding in. The old swing his father built and Miles later helped him to restore sat as a relic in the wild grass.

The image from that day was one of many during his life that Miles never forgot. He painted it as an homage to the days that only now existed as dreams. He gave it to Bryan and Molly because hanging the picture in his own house, where he would see it every day, was just too taxing given his difficulty in letting go of his childhood home, and his father.

Before wrapping the painting for Bryan and Molly, in the bottom left corner he added a shadow in the wild grass. Miles never made up his mind about who it was standing out of frame. Some days he believed the shadow was of himself, on that fateful afternoon, taking one last good look around. Other days that shadow was his dad.

Miles sipped from his Sam Adams. The last tendrils of orange and pink light slid behind the darkened heights of the treetops. Out of the approaching night came the calls of insects, the chirps and the clicks, joining together with the curtain call songs of the many birds settling in for the night. Miles sighed a relaxing sigh, settling into the wooden backing of his seat.

The flick of a lighter caught his attention. Bryan set a lit citronella candle on the wooden railing of the porch in front of them.

"So, Miles, what good news have you brought me?"

When asked, Miles was already deep into inhaling the sweet evening air, perfumed with the scent off the citronella. He took another sip from the bottle. "Good news?"

"Like I said earlier: you never call me anymore. And you certainly haven't invited me out to meet you, not in a while anyway. So I figured you have something to share. So what's going on?"

Miles could only see the hint of his brother-in-law's face with the help of the flickering candlelight. Everything else was obscured in inky shadows. This gave Miles comfort. It was much easier to open up and speak truths when he couldn't be seen, or see who he was speaking to. It was like opting to remain behind the screen during a confession rather than facing the priest head on.

"I don't know what's happening to me," he said. He could feel the weight of Bryan's stare linger through the dark. "When you told me about the gallery show . . . I'll admit, it scared the hell outta me. I hadn't done anything, barely even touched a pencil since Steph died. I didn't know how I was going to come up with anything new."

The unnerving presence of a mosquito whined at a high pitch in his left ear. He swatted and it flew off, for the moment.

"You can always put up old stuff, Miles. It was never about you making anything new. It was about you getting yourself back out there. Hang a couple of the old paintings like Molly was talking about, some of the ones from your personal collection no one's ever seen before. That's all you need. Couple of those and you got yourself a show. Everything's new to those who haven't seen it." He paused, probably dealing with a mosquito. "Hopefully this whole thing will bring that old spark back—get you coming up with new stuff."

"But that's just it," Miles said. "I hadn't had any ideas; probably would have wound up using those old paintings. But then . . . it just happened."

In the great pause, Bryan didn't ask *What happened?*, instead opting to just let Miles talk. Miles thought he could feel Bryan's eyes narrow in question through the dark.

"I started getting these . . . pictures . . . these flashes in my head."

He heard Bryan shift in his chair. Maybe uncomfortably.

"I know it sounds crazy, but when they happen . . . all I want to do is draw. I draw what I see."

A few more mosquitos whined near his head, the citronella candle had begun to fade. The short wick shrinking into the pool of melted wax.

"Anything good?" he asked.

At first Miles wasn't sure he heard the question correctly. In light of the strangeness he was dealing with, and now openly sharing, he expected Bryan to react with a coarse dose of skepticism. Maybe even challenge his sanity (hell, it wouldn't be the first time, from either of them), but none of that was happening. It made Miles feel good.

"Well, actually," said Miles of his newest works, "none of it's too bad." Of course he wasn't going to delve into the details. Bryan didn't need to know how the new pictures were made. Suspension of disbelief only goes so far. Flashes of images in his mind was one thing, drawing these pictures with his eyes closed as if he were being possessed was taking up residency in an entirely different ballpark.

He could hear Bryan take a long pull off his bottle. The smack of his lips freeing from the glass mouth. The fizzing and settling of the amount still left inside. Then, Bryan said, "I see what's going on here, Miles."

Miles drained the last of his Sam Adams. He wiped his mouth. "Oh yeah?"

"Sure," said Bryan. By this point the wick in the citronella had long exhausted itself, only the rising smoke from the dead candle continued to waft. They were sitting in pitch black with an ocean of stars overhead. "For the last eight months I've talked to you like a brother."

Because you kind of are, Miles thought.

"I've coddled you since my sister died. I'm not saying I regret it or that I shouldn't have—we've both been through a lot of pain. But now I see it." Bryan cleared his throat. "For a long time I've waited for you to get to where you are now. I think deep down somewhere you wanted this to be sooner. But now I see it. I also hear how different you sound."

Doctor Andrews had said something similar. He had picked up on a change in Miles as well.

You look different, sound different.

You walked in here differently.

It's like you woke up.

Woke up.

Bryan went on. "I was wondering at first if I was wrong to book the Garland show, but now I see it was just what you needed."

Miles straightened up in his chair. "Wait a sec. Are you taking credit for all of this?"

Bryan let out a throaty belch that caused a momentary disquiet among the chirping insects. "You're welcome."

Miles asked point blank: "So, you don't think I'm crazy?"

"Miles, if you're working again, I don't care if you're seeing visions in your head or the Virgin Mary in your toast. If you're working to get back out there and be happy then that's what matters to me."

They sat in silence for a few more moments under the stretch of infinite black. An owl hooted. Somewhere an old dog barked, to which another neighborhood dog howled. Miles swatted at a few mosquitos tracing close by. With the citronella out and the smoke from the snuffed out wick dissipated, the tiny pests began swarming in shifts.

The longer he sat there thinking about it, the more Miles found what he wanted to say. There was one finer detail he could mention.

"There's a woman . . ." he said. It felt funny to say, igniting a bit of guilt once it was out for Bryan to hear. "She just moved into the apartment upstairs."

His brother-in-law was quick to mount that particular pony.

"A woman huh?" said Bryan. Then: "Is she hot?"

"Relax," Miles said. "It's not—"

"Miles, let me tell you something."

Due to the insistence and growing volume in Bryan's voice—and that Miles wasn't yet hearing judgment—he yielded any attempt to explain himself.

"Stephanie was my sister. We didn't always get along, especially when we were young. Actually, if you can believe it, she was a pain in the ass. But I tell you, anyone ever did wrong by her and I was there."

There was an interlude where all the while Miles wasn't sure what direction this was going.

"I would have done anything to protect her," Bryan went on to say. "And I know you would've too.

"I know you blame yourself for that night. I know because for a long time I blamed myself, too. It's taken me nearly this long to deal with it, even longer to get over her. But getting over her doesn't mean *forgetting* her. You get me?"

Bryan didn't allow time for an answer.

"Her death doesn't mean you have to stop living. If you've found someone—"

"That's just it." Miles now had to interrupt. "I don't know what this is. I only just met her." He paused. "It's . . . confusing."

"Well, what do you know about this woman?"

He thought carefully. What could he say that he knew with any real sense of certainty? There was only one thing. "That she lives upstairs."

"You're like a puppy, Miles."

"A puppy?"

"Yeah, a puppy. An excitable puppy that's just found somewhere to bury his bone." Bryan giggled at his own joke.

Miles replied, "Classy."

"It's a schoolboy crush is all," said Bryan. "Nothing to feel guilty or ashamed about."

But he did feel guilty. With Stephanie gone all this time his heart still yearned for her. She was never coming back and yet that didn't stall him or sway his feelings one bit. Only made them stronger. He'd spend the rest of his life loving her, pining for her, wanting her back, haunted by the emptiness created by her absence. There would always be her side of the bed, her seat at the table, her spot on the couch, her place next to him. Those things didn't just vanish because a person did. Stephanie was his scar.

As for his feelings towards this mysterious woman living above him . . . He didn't know what they were, couldn't form them into words or cohesive thoughts. Was that why he felt so guilty? Because even deep down inside where no one else could look and judge, he didn't know what he was admitting to himself?

"So you met this woman and don't even know her name?" Bryan said.

Miles supposed that was the one real thing he knew for sure.

"Ava," he said. "Her name's Ava."

And now he couldn't get her out of his head. The guilt worsened. The mere consideration of this stranger invading his mind with a strength and regularity that threatened the presence of his deceased wife made him want to claw at his thoughts as if they were a tangible thing. Mental real-estate was limited and precious, and he was becoming a little worried that Ava was taking over more ground than Stephanie occupied.

A loud *thwack* pierced the night—a hand striking flesh.

"Goddamn mosquitos," Bryan muttered. "I'm getting eaten alive out here. Let's head in."

They both stood and made their way towards the light of the kitchen, bringing along their empties. Bryan had just grabbed the handle for the backdoor when Miles stopped a few steps behind.

"Christian," he said.

Bryan hesitated opening the door. "Huh?"

"I never told you, but if Steph and I were able to have children of our own . . . she was convinced the first one would've been a boy. We wanted to call him Christian."

Bryan turned to face Miles, only his silhouette could be made out in the light from inside the house. He tried the name out for size. "Christian." His head nodded. "It's a good name."

He didn't get back to the apartment until well after ten. Before leaving, Miles kissed Lily goodnight as she slept peaceful in her crib and thanked Bryan and Molly for having him over. Going home he took his time, snaking through winding hillside roads till meeting the onramp for 17 West.

Listening to the wind rush through the open windows, feeling the thickening chill of the cooling air on his arms as the truck coasted alone, dense fog rolling in off the riverbed, turning the night an eerie shade of orange against the lit lampposts off the side of the highway that lined the three-lane path going northbound.

There was a clean fragrance to the fog once it enveloped him, a scent like that of a fresh spring rain that begins the thaw. With no one else on the road, Miles had that momentary sense that he was the only one left in the world. Occasionally his thoughts drifted to Lily, on still wishing that he could've been a father. He would have made a great dad, he thought. But those thoughts had to be pushed aside in his attempts to pay attention to the lanes vanishing about ten feet in front of his headlights in the thick blanket of fog.

No lights were on in the upstairs apartment when he pulled into the driveway. Miles made a quiet exit, shutting the driver's side door slowly, carefully, purposefully neglecting to hit the automatic lock button on his key fab. He didn't want the noise to disturb the woman upstairs.

The backdoor into the breezeway tended to require a forceful slam to engage the handle lock, but he managed the task with a very calculated effort that produced very little sound at all.

After flipping on the table lamp next to the couch in the living room, he had every intention of setting his keys and wallet down on the stand and going off to bed. He wasn't going to need anything to help him sleep. The day, and everything that came with it, had proven exhausting. But in a good way, a *great* way. Miles felt accomplished, felt a beaming of pride. Between his session with Andrews, and his evening with Bryan and Molly and Lily, he felt he'd gotten a lot off his mind. He felt refreshed. Now all he wanted was to close his eyes.

But just as he was about to cut the light it sounded like someone had knocked on the front door.

The rapping had been so gentle the first time he wasn't sure he really heard anything at all. Then it came again. Harder.

The exhaustion that had been dogging him vanquished. His pulse quickened. It wasn't the matter of someone being out on the porch that was concerning—he knew exactly who it had to be—but that he never heard her come down the stairs.

With his light being on and visible though the small half-circle window at the top of the front door, he knew he couldn't just ignore her knocking. He had no good reason not to answer.

And so he took a breath, and shook away his nerves, before opening the door to her.

That feeling again. It hit hard and fast. First it was his stomach dropping, akin to the effect of standing inside an elevator as it drops quickly. Then came the buzzing in his chest; pinpricks spreading all over, traveling the length of his arms, gooseflesh down the notches of his spine. It was as if every single hair on his skin were made to stand by an electric current. Every cell in his body glowing bright and hot. An awakening.

Woke up.

The duration was hardly long-lasting, just enough to be noticeable after the door opened. Miles found himself short of breath. His head swimming in a fogbank. One hand reached for the doorframe for balance while the other spread over his chest.

"Are you all right?" Ava asked.

And just like that, her voice acknowledging him, the wave of dizziness and the tingling of pins and needles in his chest began to wear off. The only trace of the spell that remained in wake was the resulting sweat that broke out on his forehead. He took a shaky step backwards, trying to maintain his returning balance. If it were ever in doubt before, it was now no longer a question in his mind that this woman, this stranger who came to his building out of thin air it seemed, was more than she let on.

Whatever effect she was having on him, he hadn't a clue. But he knew it meant something.

"Miles?"

"Yeah," he finally said. He blinked several times and rubbed his brow to clear the cobwebs. "Just . . . feelin a bit funny is all. Tired I think." It felt like his blood sugar had taken a dive. The back of his mouth was dry, tongue thick with pasty saliva. "I was just . . . uh . . . on my way to bed."

It was then he noticed she was in the same outfit from the night before. The same simple white tee and black yoga pants that stopped at her shins. Neither had so much as a smudge or look of wear to them. The stark colors were pristine, and both fit her shape perfectly. Miles guessed she either wasn't well enough off for diversity in her wardrobe and owned a closet full of the same thing, or she was on the run and hadn't packed more than what she was wearing. She was also barefoot.

"Why are you here?" he asked.

"I heard you come in," she said. "You've been gone most of the day. I thought I'd check on you."

What an odd thing to say. He didn't know how to respond other than to say he was fine, and it bordered on being rude, giving her the brush off when it came out. Now that the bizarre feelings had passed, he'd had the wherewithal to put his guard up. There was so much uncertainty regarding this woman.

"But you're not fine," she said. That had taken him off guard, and before he could say anything to the contrary, she pressed deeper. "You miss her."

Miles felt his face redden with a simmering annoyance. It was hard to speak, but he managed through the catch that hit in his throat. "I'm sorry?"

"Your wife," said Ava. "You miss her."

Miles was awestruck, and not in a good surprise kind of way. He felt violated. Naked. Who was this woman to come around proclaiming personal stuff like that? Who did she think she was? More importantly, how could she possibly know? Miles was finding it harder to breathe, his frustrations working themselves up. Ava's face contorted to reveal a deep regret, realizing perhaps how much she was upsetting him.

"I'm sorry." She gestured with her chin. "You still wear your ring."

As she said that, Miles realized he was twisting the silver band on the third finger of his left hand. That happened sometimes, not so much anymore. He used to catch himself playing with his wedding ring back when the wounds were still fresh. Now, it was more a subconscious habit, like biting your fingernails. He wondered how long he had been doing it, and it dawned on him that it wasn't much of a puzzle for Ava to figure out. Here he was, living by himself and wearing a wedding ring. She needn't be a rocket scientist to put two and two together that something bad happened.

"It's fine," he said. "Don't apologize."

She put on a wan smile, seemingly for his sake.

"It's . . ." he sighed, allowing the anger that had been billowing inside to blow over. "It's been a long day."

Having had enough and ready for bed, Miles was about to thank her for stopping by and then end with saying goodnight when something small and dark came rushing toward his face. About the size of a dollar bill folded in half, the thing looked to be a giant moth. It came into the apartment from over Ava's right shoulder, looking like it had come right out of her hair. Miles flinched out of the way. The creature flapped its wings in the direction of the small light on the stand, setting down on the lampshade.

There he could see it wasn't a moth at all.

"It's okay," said Ava. "It's just a butterfly."

The creature flexed its wings and then came off the shade, affixing itself to the lower neck of the lamp, wings rising slowly in anticipation of taking flight again as Miles neared it. He studied its fat body, its wings resembling that of a monarch.

"It's a Painted Lady," he said. The same kind he and Stephanie had once kept as a caterpillar and released into the white skies and windy day of an uncertain future over a decade ago. The same kind that had crossed over his windshield just a day ago. A drawing of a Painted Lady also existed in the Winston sketchpad that lay on the coffee table just behind him. The species wasn't rare by any means, but with this new one perched on the lamp, he'd never seen so many in such a short period of time.

It was as if he were drawing them in.

Or it was her, Miles thought. She brought it with her. That would better explain the creature being out at such a late hour.

"Some people consider them good luck," said Ava, who remained in the doorway. "Like ladybugs."

"My wife . . ." Miles found himself saying, watching the antennae of the insect feel around the lamp's neck, ". . . she loved this kind of butterfly. She always had a weird relationship with them. They'd always hang around her."

He laid a hand out flat underneath the insect and slowly lifted. The Painted Lady however didn't have a wish to be captured or held; it lifted away in a flurry of beating wings. Miles lost sight of it after it moved beyond the passageway between the living room and dining room.

"A part of her that's been transferred to you, perhaps," said Ava. "Maybe now it is you who has become a magnet."

A comforting thought. Sweet even. Miles didn't expect that from her. "Goodnight, Miles."

By the time he turned around she was gone, the screen door latching closed.

"Goodnight," he said.

Miles locked up and turned off the light in the living room. All the while he never heard his neighbor climbing the stairwell that was set behind the back wall of his living room. Didn't hear the front door upstairs open and close. Didn't once hear her footsteps over the floor above.

He wondered where the Painted Lady was as he made his way to his bed through the dark. He half-expected to feel it flutter by his neck or hair or bounce off his face. There was a lot on his mind as he stripped down and climbed underneath the sheets.

Maybe now it is you who has become the magnet.

Maybe.

These were the thoughts that lulled him off to sleep.

He never should have left.

He didn't want to, but Stephanie was persistent. Bed-ridden the last two days with a fever that even the most potent over-the-counter drugs proved worthless in subduing for too long, she admired his reluctance to leave her side, but still insisted. He'd already canceled one appearance in Elmira the day before. He had been booked to speak to a group of art majors at the liberal arts college. She didn't want him missing out on his short trip to Scranton also because of her.

He stressed that the appearance—following a two hour drive south, mostly through construction once beyond the PA border—wasn't all that important. He was to be included on a panel at the Everhart museum, a panel of artists and sculptors and designers native to upstate New York and northern Pennsylvania. They would be speaking about upcoming student options and programs to engage specific art majors attending the major state universities during the following spring semesters. Exciting stuff.

Surely his colleagues would be fine without him. No one would even miss him. Just a courtesy call to her brother and Bryan would have things taken care of.

Stephanie remained steadfast. "Really, Miles, it'll be fine. It's just for a day." She then suffered a phlegmy coughing fit with numerous gasps through a plugged nose; her nostrils were red, crusty, and sore looking. Her voice was filtered through the nasal blockage. A gleam of sweat at her temples from the fever was just another sign of how fine she really wasn't. Her temperature fluctuated through the afternoon, in between doses of acetaminophen.

"I just feel awful leaving you like this," he said, sitting down on the bed.

She offered up the best smile she could, grimacing at what was all the aches and pains screaming out of her body as she rolled from her left side onto her back. "You won't be missing out on anything here," she said. "I'll still be right here and—" she sneezed out a nasty string of gunk and deposited it as ladylike as she could into a nearby wad of tissues that'd already been previously used "—and exactly the same when you get back."

He swept a few sweaty strands of hair off her forehead. "Well, when you put it like that . . ."

She flashed him a dirty look.

"Are you sure?" he asked, knowing her answer already. He was only asking for his own sake at this point. Trying to alleviate guilt.

"Already got my hot tea, tissues, and Tylenol." She sniffed back hard, the sound of something weighty and thick released from the back of her nasal passages and landed at the back of her throat. She swallowed twice. "Just gotta ride it out."

He never should have left.

Soon as he parked in the overcrowded lot of the Everhart he tried calling home on his cell but she hadn't answered. Probably asleep. He tried again. Once he got inside and swept up in the stuffy atmosphere there wouldn't be many opportunities to slip away and dial home. The panel wasn't happening for another hour but many of the art crowd he spent time coming up with over the years would be eager to get a quick meal and catch up. The line rang through six times and then the machine picked up.

A bad feeling set in.

He tried to convince himself that there was nothing to worry about. But that wasn't working. A nagging little worry, piercing all rational thought, kept reminding him of the green van.

Why couldn't she have just picked up? He just needed to hear her voice.

He tried calling a third time. The machine answered.

Despite all attempts to rid his mind of the worst possible scenarios, he wouldn't stop picturing the rusted out minivan, painted the ugliest shade of green. It had been parked curbside about fifty feet back in his rearview mirror when he backed out of the driveway onto Edgebrook. In a neighborhood of immaculate houses, clean yards, and shiny SUVs to fit the whole family, this van stood out like a cancerous mass. A conclave dent in the front bumper on the passenger side ate up most of the face like the flesh-eating virus. Next to that a hairline crack went up through to the headlight. He'd only been able to see the crack because it was white and the headlight itself was spider-webbed. A long piece of what looked to be black metal twine was wrapped through a makeshift hole in the bumper (that was also rusting in addition to being loose) and looped inside the dented grill to keep the bumper itself from dragging on the asphalt.

He'd only seen the van for a few seconds before pulling away, but it had made an impression. Every so often a picture of it poked at him like a headache. A single throb, impossible to ignore, needling him above his right eye.

Once the panel ended he tried calling home again. He was answered by the machine asking him to leave a message. Quite resolved with the near certainty that he was overreacting, but totally fine with that, Miles excused himself from the gathering afterwards and bolted out of the lot headed for I-81 North.

An hour and forty-one minutes later—having gone nearly eighty-five along the entire length of interstate, even where common speed traps existed before and after the New York State line, the welcome sight of Serling Oaks, along with its suburbs filling in the bowl of the valley community tucked away in the rolling hills of the Adirondacks, came into view around a bend where the roadside pines and oaks came to an end.

It was another ten minutes down the highway, passing the heart of town on the outer rim, before he reached his exit. The setting sun cast blinding rays of final light before slinking below the cap of the westward hills. The sky put out an ominous orange and red. Miles tried to phone home while taking the off ramp but found his nerves too rattled to dial on the touch-screen. The button for the voice-command feature for dialing was too small for his thumb to activate.

He never should have left.

The moment that confirmed this awful intuition came when the flashing lights could be seen through the trees a block away from home. There were at least three sets of whirling reds and blues along with a few blinking whites that could be made out as he turned off the connecting road. In the dusk the lights were merging. Attempting to count the amount of emergency vehicles that looked to be parked on his road proved to be a fruitless task. Panic was setting in.

After turning onto Edgebrook, he applied the brakes at the sight of many of his neighbors gathered up against orange police barricades blocking off access. A few of them turned and shielded their eyes at the bright warmth of his headlights. Miles shifted into park and cut the engine. He gave it a moment—trying to convince himself that it was useless to worry without knowing, but was failing horribly—before stepping out, a hundred yards short of home.

The air was quiet. Solemnly quiet. Deathly quiet.

Thirty or so people stood facing the end of the winding road ahead, and not one of them was speaking to another.

The bright LEDs atop the emergency vehicles continued spinning and flashing, but not one of them was blaring its sirens.

Now Miles could worry. No sirens meant the worst was already over. Whatever happened had happened. There wasn't any urgency about the scene. Now, it seemed, for the men and women in their various uniforms walking about, it was all about follow-up procedures.

And just as Miles approached the flock of neighbors, a few of them turning their heads in his direction with shocked expressions of sorrow, a State Police SUV began making a slow exit from the scene. The officer in the passenger seat hopped out to move one of the sawhorses out of the way so the vehicle could pass through. The flock, like a gaggling of geese, shifted silently out of the way. After the officer reset the barricade once the vehicle was through, the lights flashed a few times and Miles caught his reflection in the windows as the SUV sped off into the night.

A sharp ringing then pierced the silence.

Next thing Miles knew he was staring up at the ceiling. Waves of cool breeze came in through the window on his right, chilling his damp skin. It was morning; the sun bright and birds squeaking and squawking. His body was clenched, muscles tight with ache. Even his teeth hurt from a clamped jaw. The bed sheets were twisted. Nothing new.

There was only enough alertness to discern the ringing—that which pulled him from his dreams—was his cell phone in his pants pocket on the floor.

"Fuuccck," he groaned and rolled to the edge of the bed.

He scrambled trying to reach onto the floor, a bubbly awareness draining away as the blood began to circulate faster. Another blatting of his phone. No telling how many times it'd rung so far. At any point it would go to voicemail.

One hand on the floor to keep steady, he finally reached his pants, bunched up far enough away that only his knees remained on the bed, the rest of his body planking off over the floor.

The ringing stopped.

By the time Miles dug through the pockets and finally freed his phone, there was an exclamatory *ding* and the screen lit up, reading: (1) NEW VOICEMAIL

He swiped his thumb over the lock-screen and dialed his inbox. He entered the four-digit pin when prompted.

The first thing he heard was the rush of what had to be the breeze off the ocean. Numerous voices were carrying on in the background. A dog barked. Seagulls nagged. Then came the raspy voice of his landlady.

"Miles? It's Evelyn." He quickly noted a pinch of alarm in her voice. "I'm calling because I just heard from Jimmy. He says no one's contacted him about renting the upstairs. Didn't you say you were hearing *noises* up there?"

Just about everything else she said he didn't get until he listened to the message a second time. Unconsciously the phone trailed away from his ear, his eyes turning upward at the ceiling, in the direction of the occupied second floor, as the rest of his body slipped off the bed and landed with a heavy thud.

The end of Ms. Hutchings's message said that her grandson would be stopping over sometime during the day to investigate the upstairs apartment. Beyond her initial concern there was no discernable giveaway in the landlady's gravelly voice as to whether she thought the situation required immediate action (like that of the law enforcement kind), or if her thinking was more on the lax side. Miles phoned her back to tell her he no longer heard anything upstairs but it rang through to her own inbox. Following the beep he quickly dissolved into a rambling, incoherent mess, eventually blaming what he heard on a family of mice that had somehow gotten in through the vents. He didn't want to bother Jimmy with the task of coming all the way over for something so trivial, instead volunteering himself to lay out a few traps smeared with peanut butter if she wanted. He then hung up.

It was entirely possible he had made things worse.

She was up there; Jimmy would find that out whenever he decided to show up. And while Jimmy wasn't the most punctual super when it came to making calls, there was now a sense of urgency in that Miles didn't know if his landlady had also contacted the local PD, who could show up any minute. Regardless of who arrived first, this wasn't going to spell out well for Ava. Most likely she would be swept away in the back of a squad car for trespassing, at the very least. And if that happened, Miles would never get to talk to her, would never get to learn her connection to all the strange things happening to him.

He had to go up there. Now. He told himself he may not get another chance.

The thought of seeing her again filled him with an unsettling mix of confusion, apprehension, and a nervous anticipation. The insides of his belly squirmed. Of the two times they'd met previously, Miles had felt an undeniable link between them that was beyond anything he'd known before. Different even to the connection he had with his wife.

Miles was denying himself. Something about her. Something he knew deep down. Afraid to admit. Afraid to confront.

But now time was running out.

He needed to get to Ava before anyone else.

The FOR RENT sign that hung on the inside of the screen door was peeled away when a gust of wind pried the latch out of his hand and the door swung away from him. Miles failed to retrieve the sign before it was carried off down the street. The sunlit morning he awoke to had given way to dark skies. Heavy raindrops started to fall as he opened the front door. Once in the stairwell he made no attempt to soften his steps up to the landing; it didn't matter if Ava heard him coming or not. Before he was in front of her door, Miles paused on the last step and composed himself.

He knocked, gently.

She didn't answer.

He knocked again, firmer this time.

He set an ear close to the door and listened for footsteps inside. He'd heard nothing above him all morning and now it was only the sounds of a steady rain drumming off the roof. The growl of thunder was far off, sounding to him like a distant train.

Again she didn't come to the door.

"Ava?" he said, knocking once more. "Ava, it's me, it's Miles. Can I talk to you for a sec?" He listened again and heard nothing inside. Was she avoiding him? Maybe she was asleep.

He knocked harder.

She didn't answer.

From his left pocket he pulled out the spare keys the landlady entrusted him with. He had grabbed them on his way out to unlock the front door off the porch but it had been open (Miles wondered if the door had been relocked since the last time he'd let himself in). He felt really uncomfortable using the key labeled APT2 to get into the apartment, even on someone who wasn't supposed to be there. Though the key hadn't worked when he'd gone up before.

He resigned to knocking again, mentally pleading for her to make this easy on him and come to the door. "Ava?"

Silence.

Miles again regarded the keys. The booming thunder was closer, forceful enough to rattle the walls of the stairwell. He bit his bottom lip, squeezed the keys until he felt the sharp ridges dig into the tender meat of his palms, reddened indentations left behind. She had to hear him standing out there, even over the intensifying rain and crackles of thunder. He wondered how he could justify using the keys.

Then it came to him.

"Ava?" he said, voice dripping with concern. "Is everything all right?" Nothing.

"Are you hurt?" He doubted anything was wrong with her, physically anyway, but he needed a good cover story in case he needed to explain—to her or to the police—why he broke into the apartment.

"Ava?" He gave an appropriate pause. Thunder stretched out across the heavens. "I'm coming in. Just wanna make sure you're all right."

The key for APT2 slid perfectly into the lock, just as before. It was when Miles had gone to turn the key the last time that the door wouldn't open, as if the bolt had refused to budge. He expected the same to happen this time, and would have felt a wave of relief over not having to break in.

Not so this time. The lock retracted, clicking over without requiring the smallest bit of force.

"Fuck," he sighed, closing his eyes.

He peeked his head inside. "Ava?" The first night he laid eyes on her, when this very door flew open on him standing out on the stoop, the light from within the apartment had been blinding. But now no lights were on, the living room empty.

He flipped the light switch and the single bulb housed in the glass casing over the middle of the room remained out. Either dead or the power had been shut off since Lou, the previous tenant, moved out.

"Ava?"

Miles checked each room, all of them bare. He was alone.

The power was still on in his own apartment. The lights flickered and hummed during a particularly brilliant lightning strike. Rain pelted the windows. Miles settled into his red recliner, defeated. The woman upstairs was gone. Taken with her was any hope he had of learning what was going on. And since she had been somewhat of a catalyst behind the strange things affecting him, he wondered if her sudden vanishing act meant that it was all over. Were there going to be anymore dreams? Would he ever again feel the brush of his wife's skin against his? Looking down on the floor, the Winston sketchbook lying there made him also question if he would ever feel another rush of inspiration come over him, that feeling of awakening within, the pins and needles feeling. Would he ever draw again? Forget having enough work for the exhibition the following week, with Ava now gone did it mean his life was going to recede back into drifts of wallowing through the mundane?

Whoever this woman was, her brief existence in his life had changed him, started to bring him back.

He bent down and picked up the sketchbook, noticing while he did that sitting on top of one of the vertical blinds was the Painted Lady that had come in the night before. Ava had let it in.

The butterfly sat eerily still, its wings downturned. Miles had the unsettling thought that it was perched up there watching him.

Miles flipped through the pages of the Winston, stopping to study a few of his old, meaningless practice sketches. Then he came to *The Storm*. Around the binding rings remained loose scraps of the page previously torn loose—the page containing the twisted visage of the scarred man. That picture was now facedown (literally) on the carpet half underneath the coffee table.

Thunder crashed overhead. Miles's eyes went back to the storm. Something in the back of his mind clicked.

"Wait."

He flipped the page to the next drawing—*The Painted Lady*.

He looked up. The butterfly remained poised on the cusp of the tall blind.

Miles gasped. "Holy shit."

If his line of thinking was correct, that the bundle of his anxieties and pain had essentially made him a scarred man, then all three of his most recent pictures—ones made since he had given up his art career—were there. Unbelievably, impossibly, but undeniably there, existing outside the confines of the page. The scarred man being himself. The storm raging outside. The Painted Lady looking down on him.

And there was one other picture. One he had forced himself long ago to put far out of mind after he hid it away down in the cellar eight months ago.

A painting that explained his connection to the woman gone missing.

The once occasional drip of water down in the dark of the cellar had become much steadier with the ongoing rain. The smell had also intensified. Pungent dankness wafted up the stairs to where he stood out in the breezeway. Miles had spent so much time and effort blocking out what was on the canvas stashed down in the back corner of the basement that, until the thought occurred to him, he'd almost forgotten it existed. It was on the same level as convincing yourself of a lie; telling yourself the same thing over and over until soon enough you start to believe what isn't true.

To the chorus of puddles forming on the concrete floor, he descended the stairs, stopping to reach for the drawstring attached to the bulb hanging at the bottom. The musty, damp air left a stale taste on his tongue.

Through the open entranceway on the left, Miles felt water soaking through his shoes after a deep splash in a divot in the floor. He found the string for the second light and pulled on it. The pale yellow light illuminated the six storage bins stacked on pallets along with the shallow and deep puddles all along the floor leading back to the shadows of the far left corner.

The sudden startup of the sub-pump out by the stairs put a startle into Miles's heart. He sloshed through the shallowest spots of gritty water, working a careful path toward the back corner where a dull shine reflected back at him.

There was a third drawstring and light somewhere among the pipes and wires in the ceiling, but since Miles didn't frequent the backend of the cellar often, except the one time to stash the black garbage bag containing the painting he was after, he didn't know where to find it and had to, instead, go by the light off the screen of his cell.

Ducking under a vent shaft, he was there. The walls meeting in the corner were riddled with slimy black cracks and spots stained yellow and brown where old water leaks had permeated through the rock.

The black garbage bag rested standing against the corner. It was slick all over with beaded drops. Miles snatched it up quick and tore away the plastic, pulling in opposite directions where the red synch at the top had been knotted, fearful the picture inside had been irrevocably damaged.

Not only hadn't the painting been harmed in any way, the woman's pristine face, her mocha-colored skin, even her raven-black hair swarmed all around by butterflies that had been a last minute touch, had been so exact it delivered a most terrifying truth, a shot that confirmed Miles's wild revelation.

His art was coming alive.

Once he was past the shock of it all, Miles returned to his apartment. Stepping inside the kitchen with the painting in hand, he was surprised to find the woman on the canvas was now standing in his living room, waiting for him.

In the time spent away from The Work, the artist is rejuvenated and returns with a renewed sense of purpose. A strive to finish.

He stared at her. His eyes traced over the lines of her that his hand once etched into the canvas. He noted the meek look in her ordinary, and beautiful face. Her lips were slightly parted, on the cusp of maybe uttering his name in surprise once she saw him. She wore the same crisp white shirt, the same fitted black pants. Plain. Unassuming. He watched her breathe in, how her slim stomach inflated slightly with air. She was alive—real—because of him. He understood their connection now, but not yet the purpose of it all.

She stared at him. All the while neither of them said anything to each other he wondered if she knew everything going through his mind. She'd shown a propensity of wielding such an extraordinary ability; her heightened power of perception of him likely derived from her essentially being a part of him. If she knew what he was thinking then she knew his nerves were on edge; she knew her mere presence turned his guts into a twisted, quivering bundle. Part of this because he couldn't get a bead on what she was thinking. She seemed to know everything about him—he got that from her dark eyes alone. But other than that he sensed nothing from her.

He was also nervous because . . . he needed her.

Miles set the painting down on the kitchen floor then closed the gap between them. Ava's eyes faltered a bit but she maintained her spot on the living room carpet. He could only keep his gaze for so long before his own eyes lowered.

He mumbled something, something that he thought sounded too stupid to speak aloud. She didn't respond. He didn't know if she heard and quickly got agitated enough to just say it outright.

"Why is this happening to me?"

She started by the sudden rise in his volume. He sighed, his face turning apologetic. He asked in a much quieter, calmer tone. "Can you tell me anything?"

Her eyes met his again.

"Please," he said. "What am I supposed to do?"

The eyes studying him changed. Her pupils looked to narrow, her deep brown irises focused, homed on him. There was something certain going on in her mind that he wasn't privy to, until her lips started moving.

"You still have work to do."

The intensity of the thunderstorm—*his* thunderstorm—reached its apex around the time Miles sat down at his makeshift work area. Lined up on the coffee table were his acrylics and a few brushes of different varieties. He also had with him his freezer bag of pencils along with a handful of kneaded erasers and a sharpener. The Winston sketchpad remained closed. Ava handed him a brand new canvas out of the Michael's shopping bag. The pencil he picked up was the gnawed on Ticonderoga he had started the most recent drawings with.

The angle of the rain shifted with the wind. The walls groaned, the wild gusts threatening to snap the beams like they were old brittle bones.

Ava pulled the shade off the small lamp next to the couch, casting a wider, brighter light on the canvas with the exposed bulb.

Miles was set to begin. He held the tip of the pencil a hair over the canvas in his lap, focused and waiting. Not only did he have no idea what picture would dawn in his mind, he didn't know how many it would take before he finished the work Ava claimed he still had ahead of him. He also had the suspicion he was no longer drawing for the art show.

Once everything in the room was set, a steady pummeling of rain tapping on the windows and walls, Ava sat in the red recliner across the table from him.

"You've mourned your wife's death for too long," she said. "But you have never confronted it."

He regarded her with a pointed brow. "And you want me to draw a picture about it?"

Ava ignored his question. Her words retained the same formal cadence, her voice the same steady, even tone that helped to lull him. "When you got home that night, what did you see?"

It took Miles a long moment to relax and give himself over to serious consideration of her question. Once he settled in and resigned to closing his eyes and lowering himself slowly into that dark well of his memory, the images of his neighbors standing around the police barricades, where emergency lights flashed and flickered off the windows of all the nearby houses on the street, where they stood surrounded by an eerie disquiet, bubbled up to the surface, unleashing a wealth of emotions threatening to do more than just rise up, but crush him from within.

His jaw trembled. "There was a blockade set up in the middle of the road." Behind his closed eyes he could see it perfectly. The rickety sawhorses, orange with paint chipping and the acronym for the Serling Oaks Police Department stenciled in inky block text over the crossbeams. "There were so many faces that turned to look at me. By their faces I think some of them knew. They just didn't say anything. They didn't want to be the ones to tell me."

"You saw someone you knew." Her words came to him from a distance, soothing, echoing as if she were speaking from the far end of a long empty hall. Dreamlike.

"It was Cleveland," Miles said. His own voice seemed to be coming from that same place far away. It didn't feel like he was speaking at all. Like a narrator in a film.

The police SUV passed through the crowd of spectators, driving away from the scene on Edgebrook. Miles watched it follow the bend out of sight when an officer he recognized among the many milling about approached the barricade. Cleveland was a veteran of over sixteen years, and also happened to be one of Miles's neighbors from across the street. A stocky man who usually carried himself with an air of gentle cheeriness, when Cleveland summoned Miles over it was apparent in the black man's drooping jowls and downturned eyes that the worst had happened.

Miles was escorted up the street through the area heavy with emergency personnel and traffic. All the way he had been asking for the specifics but Cleveland wasn't answering. Not until they were past the yellow crime scene tape surrounding the house and reached the front walk.

That's when Miles saw the image that gutted him, the sight of which flashed in his mind as if snapped with an old Polaroid.

"He got in through that window," said Cleveland.

Miles described what he saw in the flash. "Next to the front door on the left was a window. It was part of the frame, about six and a half feet tall. We never worried that anyone would try to get in through it because it was so thin."

As he spoke, the hand with the pencil started moving. The pencil tip swept quickly and decisively over the woven white surface.

Glass was sprinkled all over the inside marble floor and out on the small stone landing. Not a piece remained in the window frame. Where there were gatherings of glass there were also numbered yellow cards—evidence markers—cataloguing the scene. Two officers nearby, unaware of Miles being there, continued to work, snapping pictures.

Cleveland's large and warm hand gripped and squeezed Miles's left shoulder. "I'm so sorry, Miles."

"Where is she?" Miles blurted out. Fresh tears stung in his eyes.

"Miles, she's not—"

He shouted. "*Where is she?*"

The two officers snapping pictures stopped.

To see the infliction of pain and surprise in Cleveland's face reflected only a small percentage of the misery ripping Miles apart at the seams. Cleveland's own eyes were stricken with tears, his emotions betraying the sturdiness he was attempting to maintain as part of his job. When he was finally able to answer Miles, he had managed to get himself under firm control.

"She's not here," he said. "Her body's . . . already been removed and transported downtown . . ." He mumbled over the last details.

A tear managed to slip out and paused on the slope of Miles's cheek. The trail of the tear was hot, burning his skin. "Who would do this? Who would just break into a house with a cop living across the street?" He looked away from the numbered yellow markers and looked Cleveland in the eyes with a fiery glare. "Did you catch him?"

He could tell Cleveland had bit down hard on his tongue.

"He shook his head at me," Miles said to Ava. He was deep into the trance, his hand directing the pencil, never thinking she probably knew everything he was telling her already. "He said they didn't know much. They didn't think there was a motive outside of it being a desperate person trying to get at some money.

"They found our safe sticking out from under the bed. He must've tried to get the combination from her . . . but she didn't give it." He was trembling, struggling to speak. "They believe he either found out she had dialed 911 when he broke in, or he panicked after he strangled her . . ."

Saying those words brought on immediate tears.

"They didn't think he meant to . . . They think he lost control. The safe was still on the floor of the bedroom when they arrived and found her. He was long gone."

Miles felt himself come awake. He was back in the living room of the apartment. The vision in his head burned off. He was looking right at Ava. The rain now a gentle shower. Quiet thunder banked off the hills.

"It was not your fault, Miles."

His eyes traveled down to the canvas propped against his knees.

The window that once fit in the thin slat to the left of the front door, reduced to shards and pebbles spread out over the smooth surface of the stone landing, had made a flawless transition to the canvas in pristine strokes of monotone graphite. Captured in all of its horror exactly as it appeared in his vision.

It was one thing to see this dreadful image in his head as part of some poignant memory, but seeing the moment when he knew his wife was dead before anyone had said it, brought to life by use of his own hand left him sickened.

"It was not your fault."

He knew that to be a lie.

"You were not there," Ava continued. "You cannot blame yourself."

He'd heard that reasoning before, from Cleveland, from Bryan, from Doctor Andrews. But there was something in the details of Stephanie's death that he never shared with any of them because of the enormous guilt wracking him from the moment he'd left her that day on his trip to Scranton.

"I felt it," said Miles, dabbing his chest. He could still clearly picture that nasty green van with its dented front bumper, the white hairline crack running through the headlight, as it sat parked against the curb in his rearview after he pulled out onto the road. "I knew something wasn't right about that van the moment I saw it. It gave me this . . . awful feeling. And I never did anything about it."

It was true that he hesitated upon seeing the van in his mirror, but, eventually, he drove off. His greatest regret.

"A hunch," said Ava. "That's all you had."

"If I had just checked it out myself, or called Cleveland to—"

"You can't think like that, Miles." A silence descended, and in that time not a single drop of rain hit against the windows nor a rumble of thunder over the hills could be heard. The storm—*his* storm—had moved on. "People in the deepest trenches of grief will dig deep and find reason to point fingers at themselves. But if you listened every time you had a bad feeling you'd never leave the house; you'd be afraid of what's out there.

"She was sick and you already felt terrible for leaving her. Had you followed your instincts that day, is it possible you may have saved her?

That it never would have happened? Yes. But you didn't. That voice in your head spoke to you, saying you were overreacting, that you were looking for any excuse not to leave. You cannot blame yourself as if you knew what would happen."

Miles carefully weighed what she said, wiping away tears under his eyes.

"You are a beautiful person, Miles. Your heart is too big to be torn with so much grief. There is still a lot of beauty in the world. Some pretty amazing things still happen. You must let yourself heal."

At this he scoffed and then, uncontrollably, it snowballed into an actual laugh that got away from him. "But *reliving* it? By drawing *pictures* of it?" He held up the sketch of the broken window to accentuate the point.

"Not by reliving it," said Ava. "By confronting it. By doing what you love most."

There came an interruption outside on the porch. They both turned in the direction of the closed front door at the sound of heavy footfalls stomping up the short stairs. The worn springs of the screen door yawned and stretched. Then came a short round of rapid knocking. Miles hopped right up to answer.

"Jimmy!"

The landlady's lanky grandson stood out on the welcome mat wringing out his drenched and worn New York Mets cap. Springs of black curls from his unkempt mane not matted down from wearing the hat coiled out over his forehead and his ears. Off the porch behind him traces of warm sunlight were emerging through the dark skies and landing in glowing strips across the neighborhood.

"Hey Miles. Got a call you've been hearing something upstairs?"

Miles couldn't take his eyes off the inches-long bush of frayed hair sticking out every which way from Jimmy's massive chin. How that wiry thatch shook when he spoke, and while he was smacking his gum.

"Uh, yeah," he said, "but to tell you the truth, Jimmy, I haven't heard anything up there in a while. I think it may have just been some mice or something."

Jimmy huffed like his time had been wasted and scratched his furry chin, flakes of dandruff drifting out like tiny snowflakes, popping and smacking his gum a few times while rolling things over in his mind. He then reached into one of the lower pockets of his oil-stained cargo shorts and took out a small ring of labeled keys. "Well, while I'm here, I may as well go up and check things out. I know my grandmother'll feel better about it."

Miles nodded with a wry grin. "Let me know if you find anything."

He closed the door and waited until he heard the sound of Jimmy climbing the steps in the hall. Miles leaned into the door, resting his forehead, closing his eyes.

"When I went up there earlier," he said, "I didn't see anything. You weren't actually living up there."

From the recliner behind him, he heard Ava say: "I am only here when you need me."

He scoffed. He walked past Ava on his way out of the living room.

"This is all to help you, Miles. Soon you'll realize it. There's not much more for you to do."

He stopped in the archway but couldn't make himself turn to look at her. "Help me?"

He heard Ava stand from the chair, but she didn't come any closer. "I know all of this is hard to understand. You had suffered and doubted yourself so much that your mind became fragile. You were more apt to believe your own sanity was slipping away had things not begun so subtle."

He laughed to himself. "For a while there, in the beginning . . . I did think I was going crazy."

Ava said nothing.

He looked back at the coffee table, where he had set down the sketch of the broken window. "Sometimes I still wonder."

"You're not crazy, Miles."

He grinned. "So says the woman from my painting."

A pause.

"We should continue," she said.

He drew his head away from the door and straightened. "I need a break. I'm going to lie down for a little while," he said. "I just can't do any more right now."

She let him go without another word.

This dream had occurred before. It was the first.

He was at the table, sitting across from the most beautiful woman. Both had their fingers wrapped around the thin stems of wine glasses half filled with red. The glasses had been drained and refilled a few times already.

He shared with her a story about how he had been stood up on a previous date with another woman. Turned out the woman learned she was pregnant with her ex-husband's child. They both laughed at his misfortune.

She asked if he'd met anyone else since.

He said no.

She made mention of how popular he was on the dating site that brought them together for this date. "There were a lot of girls interested in you. What if I'm keeping you from one of them, maybe the one you're supposed to be with?"

He took a sip of vino, waited for the kiss of the alcohol's haze to set in. "I don't think it works that way." And when she pressed him on this, he replied: "There's always a reason for things."

Their conversation took a turn down a more intimate avenue. This beautiful woman, Stephanie, too beautiful for him, leaned in, her eyes questioning, the top of her v-neck collar slipping enough to offer a tantalizing glimpse of curvy, pale skin. "So then, are you implying there's a *reason* you and I are here right now?"

That's exactly what he was saying. He was scared though. At this very early juncture in what he hoped to be a blossoming relationship with this remarkable woman, he didn't want to scare her off with some heavy-handed declaration of fate. So, with a shrug and his glass held up between them, he said: "Even the strangest things happen for a reason."

Once she caught on to the meaning that all the unusual circumstances in their separate lives had been responsible for bringing them together, she smiled, and joined in on the toast.

That's where the dream ended.

His eyes sprung open to the jolt of being shaken awake. Sitting on the bed next to him was Ava, her hand still on his shoulder.

"I'm sorry, Miles," she said, "but time is crucial."

He took in a deep breath and let it out, adjusting to being awake. "How long was I out?"

"Only about twenty minutes."

He nodded. It felt much longer than that; he would have sworn he had slept the day away. He sat up on the bed feeling completely refreshed.

"How many more do I have to do?" he asked.

There was a slight hesitation before Ava told him, "Two."

Two pictures. Miles readied himself. "Okay."

"Why do you twist your ring like that?" she said.

As it was most of the time, he didn't even realize he had been doing it.

"There are a lot of things I know because you think about them," she said. "But not this."

Now that he was made aware of it, Miles made slow, conscious turns of the ring. The band of flesh beneath featured a red circle of its own. "Just a habit," he said. He then gave one last gentle spin of the silver wedding band and assured her it was nothing to think about.

Secretly, he liked that there was one thing about him she didn't know. She asked what he remembered about the first time he met Stephanie. His mind compiled a list.

The white coat.

How the wind tossed her hair as she entered the café.

The sight of her naked throat after she removed the scarf.

The flakes of snow melting in her hair.

"I remember everything," he said. The next blank canvas sat in his lap, the same gnawed pencil twirling between his fingers.

"What were you doing just before she walked into the café?"

"Waiting," he said.

Miles closed his eyes to picture it. In seconds the dark behind his eyelids transformed into a view out onto Main Street through the dirty storefront window of the Sunset Moon Café. He was seated at a table in the small dining area, hoping to catch a glance of her walking by before she came in. A dusting of snow on the sidewalk kicked up by the wind, drifting over the glass. Some of the flakes disintegrated into droplets on the surface of the window, the rest piled on the ground at the base of the foundation.

His hands were being kept warm around a mug of steaming coffee.

"I was fidgety," he recalled, speaking outside of himself. "Nervous."

"You had gotten there early," said Ava. Her voice once again coming from down that distant hall. "You wanted to see her before she saw you."

"Yes."

The pencil in his hand stopped twirling, the point faced the canvas, the back end of the pencil pressed into the familiar soft purple depression of flesh that'd formed long ago against the first knuckle on his ring finger. Even with his eyes closed he knew where on the surface of the canvas the point of the lead would touch. Where the next picture would begin.

"Your hands are warm," she said.

In the vision, Miles grasped tighter around the mug as it flashed bright through his head. His palms and the pads of his fingers turned instantly hot. The steam rising out of the mug filled his nose with the scent of bitterness and faint coconut.

The pencil was already moving.

"Back then I only drank coffee on special occasions," he said with a soft laugh, looking back. "I didn't care for it all that much. I just thought it would calm my nerves."

"It was a distraction," said Ava. "Something to focus on while you waited."

Faster the pencil's tip scratched lines over the textured canvas. Able to sense the movement but completely unaware of what was taking up space on the surface, Miles remained back on that blustery winter's day, sitting in the café near the window. Watching.

Ava's voice, from a distance beyond place and time: "Why did you want to see her first?"

People walked by the window. None of them her.

"I wanted to know . . ." He licked at his chapped lips, his right hand moving over the canvas with fury, "I was worried she was too good for me."

He scanned both stretches of the street, searching the faces of the few strangers out walking amidst the blowing flurry on this overcast wintry day. "I had seen her picture," he said. "I was in denial that I could ever be so lucky to meet someone so beautiful."

In one time and place that Miles occupied the drawing was coming together in a maddening swirl of his hand. In another, he sat against the backing of the chair, hands still clinging to the hot mug.

Ava said, "And then you saw her."

A figure in a long white coat passed by the window. Snowdust kicked up in the wake of her boots and the tail of her coat billowing outward in the chilly gusts of February. As it was on the day, and so it was in his vision, Miles didn't feel his feet carry him into the next room, where she was coming in the front door. The bell over the door chimed. The sharp cold from outside hit his naked face.

He said, "There was this *prickling* inside my chest soon as I saw her. Something I'd never felt before."

Snowflakes in her hair and those twinkling in the air around her began to change over, catching the lights as they melted from the heat inside the doorway. Just as Stephanie unwrapped the long scarf from around her slender neck, revealing that tiny birthmark next to her throat, and looked at him, the instant recognition that she'd found him, Miles opened his eyes, his body and consciousness centering in the singular world of the apartment.

He was already looking at the canvas where there was the simple sketch of a coffee mug. A faint swirl of steam rose up from inside and dissipated inches from the top edge.

Ava was right there next to him, placing a hand on the crook of his arm. Her touch no longer incited a rash of uncertain, nearly illicit emotions from him. What he did feel from her was a sturdy measure of tranquility. Peace. Comfort. Strength.

"Holding on to faith when you can't see the reward is a hard thing to do," she said. Her hand gave his arm a gentle but firm, and certain, squeeze. "You've trusted me this far. I promise there is only a bit more. But time is running out so we must leave now."

"We're leaving?" said Miles. "I don't understand. Where are we going?"

Her eyes reflected a little bit of the sun that'd come out after the storm. "Home," she said.

There was something he needed to take care of first.

Despite a head full of reluctance and a terror seeping into his bones, Miles was determined to see this through. Even if that meant going back to the place it all started. If the dreams and the flashes and the pictures coming to life and the woman from his painting—his sub consciousness manifested, he believed—had been a recipe of directions pointing him home, then he had come far enough on the path to convince himself he couldn't stand in the way of his own progression. There was no standing still. No going back.

The end of the line was closing in.

Before leaving the apartment, he made a stop in the bathroom.

For too long he kept faith in the wrong thing. He believed the Ambien would act as his savior. They did him a favor. The red pills dulled the pangs when despair and self-judgment proved too much to handle. The quiet peace and stretches of serene, numb, uncaring bliss had been addicting.

They also nearly cost him everything when he was at an all-time low. When he should have been paying attention to the signs that told him he had taken a wayward path.

Instead he was forced to pay attention.

The pills hadn't been his savior after all.

And he had found comfort in his dreams. Knowing he could see Stephanie whenever he closed his eyes, and feel her, even if only for a few seconds, when his eyes opened again. There was no telling how long that would last.

Miles picked up the bottle off the middle shelf of the medicine cabinet, rattling the few left inside.

Watching them go down with the water in the bowl was easier than he thought. When they vanished so too did the last, lingering weight of his dependency. His first breath in the aftermath was freeing, clean.

Ava was standing at the back door, waiting when he came back out.

"Okay," he said. "I'm ready."

With the last few strokes comprising The Work, the artist weighs all factors—negative space, composition, proportion, purpose—and takes everything into consideration while in the homestretch.

Neither said anything the first ten minutes of the drive. The strip of well-manicured lawns (some littered with storm debris) and pristine houses gave way to a long stretch of pot-holed pavement and occupied businesses on the parkway. Shops, gas stations, and strip malls flanked the road. They were still another five minutes from their destination; a turnoff near the onset of the parkway going towards downtown Serling Oaks led out to a cluster of high-end neighborhoods nestled at the base of South Mountain on the outskirts.

Once a month, on the last Sunday, he would drive the eight miles back to Edgebrook Road to gather the mail from the roadside box at the end of the driveway. This routine stop was always quick. He never set foot out of the truck. He didn't do a walk-around to examine that all of the windows were intact or to make sure the lawn service he paid for was maintaining the property like they were supposed to. He simply rolled up to the curbside mailbox, put down the window, took whatever was stuffed inside to sift through later, and then peeled off. It was hard enough being that close. Knowing now they weren't going to just park twenty feet from the front door and collect the month's mail made him fidgety. Unsettled. Their slow progress through the congested end-of-the-day traffic toward the exit onto Dalton Road made him all the more anxious. They halted once again at one of the parkway's many stop-lights. Miles could see the sign with the arrow for his exit onto Dalton up ahead about fifty feet on the right. He looked to Ava; he needed to talk; the silence was driving him even madder. Teardrops slid down her face as she stared ahead.

"Ava?" he said, his unease cast away. "What's the matter?"

She blinked, a tear that had grown large in the corner of her left eye cut loose. He watched it roll all the way down her cheek, stopping at the edge of her jaw where it hung.

When she turned to him, reddened eyes glossed over with spent tears, he felt a drop hit his stomach.

"Do you want to know the future, Miles?" There was an ominous tone to her question. "I can tell you if you want to know."

He believed her. Without question she knew things—things no person had reason knowing. But then, he knew, she wasn't just some person. After the strain of the last nine months, and the many times he contemplated giving it all up, he desperately held on to any slim bit of hope that this wasn't all for nothing. And through her he could know, now, right now, what the outcome was going to be. By her count he had one picture to go, and then what? What came after that? Tomorrow? The day after? A few months, years from now? He could know. And it would be a lie to think he wasn't the least bit curious.

But saying yes to her felt like a cheat. He supposed knowing at this point when he was so close, after all he'd been through, seemed selfish.

There was also how distraught Ava was with whatever information she had. She knew all along how he was going to answer this question, he believed that too. He could only think that by her asking it would at the very least clue him in to the possibility that whatever his future had lying in wait might not necessarily be all that he was praying for.

She said this was almost over. Time was running out.

He reached over and placed his hand on top of hers that were folded together in her lap. "No," he said. "I don't want to know."

He smiled, though he didn't feel much like wanting to. It was his attempt to show her that he was all right with whatever the future turned out to be. He then gave her chin a gentle swipe, much in the way a parent would when trying to get a child to smile.

"When this is over," he said, "what happens to you?"

The picture he made of the broken window and the steaming coffee mug had been things culled from his past. Nothing in his present life had come as a result of those sketches. He didn't suddenly come upon a coffee mug or a pile of shattered glass. The Painted Lady butterfly and the storm were things that had come into his life for a short amount of time and gone. If there was a takeaway for Miles to prepare himself for, though he wanted to be wrong in the worst way, it was that this woman may not be around much longer.

He prayed she was about to tell him different.

A semblance of fondness erased the sadness that had been on Ava's face. Her tears vanished. Her eyes were clear as glass. "You won't believe me when I tell you this," she said.

He was almost afraid to ask. "And what's that?"

Her eyes widened to reveal the hint of a gleam as she went back to looking out the front window. "There will come a time, not too long from now . . . you won't even think of me."

Much as Miles wanted to protest on the spot he decided not to. He was confused and even a bit sad in her proclamation that was enough to silence him. She made it seem like he would forget all about her, and that couldn't be true.

Could it?

The lights turned green. Both lanes resumed crawling toward the intersection. Miles got into the far right lane and signaled for the exit. They resumed their stretch of quiet as he maneuvered off the parkway onto Dalton, entering a sloping and winding tree-lined stretch of road.

"A storm is coming," Ava said.

Miles looked up, but through the windshield saw only clear skies. The sun behind them had begun its slow downward arc.

Eight blocks down the road was a sign on the right for Edgebrook. The winding trail of asphalt climbed through a neighborhood of luxurious houses, properties with manicured grass, expensive lawn ornaments, plentiful gardens, trimmed hedges, and one or two along the path featured a stone fountain. But unlike the neighborhood where he occupied an apartment, there were also children here. Their toys scattered the picturesque lawns. Little ones kicked around in their Cozy Coupes along driveways, others tossed and kicked brightly colored beach balls with their parents, while older siblings chased each other around with Nerf dart guns. Miles spotted a small group of preteens engaged in a pickup game of whiffle ball.

Driving slow through the neighborhood, keeping an eye out for any excitable little ones who might suddenly dart out in front of his pickup, Miles recalled vividly the flashing emergency lights cutting through the trees on that late autumn evening. He drove through the spot where the orange sawhorses had been set up to barricade and corral everyone, keeping them at a distance from the response crew on the scene.

At the final bend in the road before 271 Edgebrook appeared, Miles prepared himself, as he'd done on all of his trips back; he held his breath like one might do when passing by a cemetery.

At the sharp incline before the hill settled out at the top was a two-story house on the right with yellow siding and a slate-colored foundation. The two-car garage underneath the house had a white door off the wide, curved driveway. Miles pulled in and parked with the truck's nose about a foot shy of the center of the garage door. The electronic opener was clipped to the visor but he never used it anymore.

Neither of them got out. They sat listening to the clicking of the engine as it cooled.

With the AC now off the air inside became sticky. Miles felt sweat pooling on his back against the leather seat. He shifted to gain a little bit of comfort.

"I've been in that apartment . . ." he said, "just trying to convince myself it was the right move. I come back here and feel guilty all over again."

He was surprised by the touch of her hand taking his still clamped to the wheel.

"You don't have to do this, Miles." Her face held that same amount of worry as before when they were stopped on the parkway. "You don't have to do anything. We can just go back, hide out in the apartment, together." There was a smidge of plea to her voice. Her eyes drifted off him. "You have to know you have a choice."

He smiled, touched deeply by her words which he also found surprising and quite out of character for her. He clasped his other hand on top of hers. "The night that I met you . . . I was about to do something . . . incredibly stupid." He thought of holding the pill bottle that night, contemplating if he could really go through with it. "I just wanted a lot of things to be over. But it was you that stopped me. I heard you upstairs. I think you wanted to save me, and you did."

He took a breath. "I had a choice then, to go upstairs and find you, or take the pills. I made my choice." He let go of her hand. "Now come on, I'll show you around."

Together they departed the pickup. The outside air momentarily felt cool against his sweating skin and the patches where his clothing adhered to his body. The noises of children from down the block were being drowned out by the buzzing of cicadas nesting in the surrounding bushes and woods. A scent of steamed blacktop sat still in the humid air. They followed the winding stone path that made up the front walk and came by the single yard light—a large glass orb covering a bulb on a black iron post. By the cloudy appearance of the orb, and the numerous spider webs snaking across the sphere, and the numerous bird droppings present, Miles doubted his lawn people were paying attention to it.

Up three stone steps to the stoop there was barely enough room for the two of them to stand while Miles fished through his keys. To their left sat a rustic decorative chair that held an old tin coffee can in the seat. There was a time when Stephanie used to plant gerbera daisies in that blue Folgers can at the beginning of every summer. Now there was only dried up soil inside the can along with a few flakes of dried up leaves and a dead spider, its legs curled up to its crusted body. On the right side, opposite the chair, was a hanging flower basket with nothing sprouting from inside. The soil inside the basket was just as old and neglected.

Behind the old chair, built into the frame of the front door, was a tall, thin window. The broken window from the picture, from the night of his wife's murder, only now fully restored.

When he caught his own reflection in it, Miles could only think of how no fingerprints had been found inside, or anywhere on the frame. Or his wife's throat. The intruder managed to not cut himself on any of the jagged shards lodged in the window while forcing through the narrow opening. The intruder, far as it concerned anyone, had been a ghost.

The door took some finagling and a little bit of muscle—in the form of ramming a shoulder against the surface—to open, the wood having swollen in the muggy heat.

A waft of dank, cool air rushed out at them as they stepped inside, reminding Miles of the stairwells at the duplex leading down to the cellar and up to the second floor unit. The modest foyer inside the house with its marble flooring reeked of staleness and musk, of air kept trapped inside for months.

Ava remained in the foyer, not saying a word while Miles walked into the living room on the right. He spent precious moments reacquainting himself with the photos of himself and Stephanie that adorned the walls—photos from their wedding just over a decade ago and other candid shots of them with other family; one had the two of them with Bryan and Molly at Liberty Island with Myra present in the form of a swollen bump under her mother's summery dress. He followed the pictures around to the dining room where there was a doorway and a pass-thru into the kitchen.

The door to a small utility closet just off the kitchen's entrance was partially open. Miles touched the golden handle and smiled upon the memory of when he and Stephanie had first been alerted to the fact that the handle on that door didn't always catch. It was on a surprisingly windy spring day shortly after they bought the house. While airing out after a long winter with all the windows open, they'd heard the door opening and slamming shut repeatedly. No matter how many times the both of them shut the door, it would come open. One of those funny little quirks that comes with a new house. Miles later installed a secondary turn lock that would keep it shut. On this walkthrough he didn't bother with it and just closed the door before crossing through the kitchen back into the foyer.

There were two sets of stairs at the backend of the foyer; the steps on the left led up to the master bedroom, bathroom, and the guest room, while the steps on the right led down to a long narrow hall where the laundry room, studio, and a separate stair continued down to the utility room in the basement and the attached garage. A sudden urge came upon Miles to go down and pay a visit to his studio.

At the mouth of the downstairs hall, he paused. Behind the closed, unmarked door facing him from the end was his studio. That simple white door was the barrier between his old life and the one he was currently existing in.

The urging—like a whispering deep in his ear—that got him to come this far continued pulling him, persuading him to go just a little farther. Much as the cold February afternoon he met Stephanie, he put one foot in front of the other towards the studio door but didn't feel himself walking. He was floating. Just short of the door he sensed a presence, no longer was he alone in the hall. He peered over his shoulder to find Ava right there with him. He never heard her approach.

"I have to go in there, don't I?" he asked.

"You've been given an exceptional gift, Miles; you can use it to choose how to remember your wife. And say goodbye."

She remained back as he took the last steps and turned the handle. The combined scent of ink, paint, and old paper greeted him as he crossed through the doorway into the studio.

The walls were white and bare. The one window on the left wall was closed, the shade drawn three-quarters to the bottom. The small fraction of natural day seeping in was enough to light the room.

Standing on different easels and leaning against the walls and numerous shelves in the room were many old works and several works-in-progress in varying stages of completion. Many of the pieces had been commissioned, some he even received advance payment for. There were acrylic paintings of sceneries, early concepts of illustrations for Little Reader books, and a few half-finished oil-based poster designs.

Among the personal collection of his Quiet Ones, Miles picked up the closest to him. It was of a nearly completed sandbox with a few mostly buried toys inside and a set of small footprints leading away. He didn't recall much about doing the picture, or abandoning it for that matter, but could see progress had stopped somewhere in the midst of applying red paint to the wood foundation of the sandbox. He turned it over to find it hadn't been titled yet.

At the far end of the room against the back wall was his desk. Simple and practical with an adjustable white top and black mesh storage shelves down the side. The white top surface that could be angled to serve as its own easel was marred with many years' worth of smudges and scuffmarks, paint drops, and more than a few random lines that'd gone off the page.

Miles took a seat in the rolling stool and ran a thumb through a stack of papers taking up residency on the corner of his desk. Old work orders, contracts not signed, a bunch of correspondence that'd come via e-mail and through the Post Office. After Stephanie died, without consideration for his responsibilities (including the jobs he'd already been hired and paid for), Miles closed up shop; there was just no desire left to create anything, the well remaining dry for a long time. Fortunately, and perhaps out of sympathy for his loss, none of the people or studios he frequently did business with pushed for their money refunded.

While glossing over all the old paperwork, he began to run the ends of his fingers over the surface marks and embedded scuffs that tainted the once plain desktop. There was a lone Ticonderoga pencil lying against the side of the paper stack. He picked it up, wielding it like he would in preparation for the next picture.

This sparked a thought. Ava's voice in his head.

You've been given an exceptional gift, Miles; you can use it to choose how to remember your wife. And say goodbye.

The clouds in his mind parted.

He knew now what was meant to be his last picture.

Why he had come home.

This wasn't like the other recent pictures. There was no sudden flash triggering a memory. No unrelenting desire came over him to put down as fast as possible an obscure image pulsing through his brain. This wasn't how Ava, *The Storm*, *The Painted Lady*, *The Scarred Man*, or the sketches of the broken window or coffee mug had come to be. But then again, when Miles sat down on the stool after adjusting his desktop to angle up thirty-five degrees and the canvas was set in place, he knew already what he was going to create.

This picture had been with him a long time.

It would take a while to finish. It had to be perfect.

This would be his masterpiece.

In order to begin he had to put out of mind that something incredible was happening to his art. He couldn't go into this final picture with a mind full of expectations. There was no guarantee anything would happen, as it had with *The Storm* and *The Painted Lady*. This new one could go the way of the others and nothing come of it. He couldn't allow himself to depend on what this picture could bring and be disappointed. Because if nothing happened there would be no greater letdown.

Before settling in for the long haul, Miles retrieved the canvas from the pickup and, sensing just how long his night was going to stretch on for, put on a pot of coffee. The can of Jamaican-Me-Crazy that was buried in the back of the freezer would do the job. The enriching scent of the coconut-infused java as it dripped into the pot made his stomach growl. After raiding the cupboards and coming up with a can of tuna (expiration date still four months away), he checked for some mayo in the fridge. Fortunately it was there, along with a few other sauces and condiments, and still had another month to go on the cap's Use-By date.

There was no fresh bread on the counter or any to defrost in the freezer so he ate the tuna by itself in a bowl. Chasing it down with a mug of black coffee did create an unusual mix of flavors in the back of his throat but, in the end, it was satisfying. After he finished scraping the bowl clean it went in the sink and then he refilled his mug—leaving the pot half full on the burner for later when he would need refueling—before retreating back down to the studio.

His focus had been so tunneled that he didn't even notice Ava was gone.

Armed with a sharpened Ticonderoga, he adjusted his seat, toyed with the bendable neck of the desk lamp that was clamped to the edge of the angled desktop, and took a few breaths before allowing the graphite tip to touch down. For a brief second Miles Greene closed his eyes, but then reconsidered and opened them. This drawing was going to be different. It wasn't going to stem from a memory that'd been filed away. This was going to come from him.

Whenever sketching a face, regardless if the subject sat for a live portrait, had been photographed, or resided mentally, Miles made a point to begin with the left eye. This went back to his first classes in art school where he was taught to determine an Origin Point. Even before he designed the shape of the subject's head, it was always this eye he began with. Because, as he learned, the Origin Point should be small. Everything should grow around it. There should also be no fine detail, just the outline. And once the left eye was down he'd then sketch the right; this helped in determining distance between them and it was easier to match in size when he could see them both with nothing else pulling his own eye away from the details. Then came the shape of the head.

A few lines were then added on to mark the placement of the nose then the mouth. Faces were always blank to start. Featureless. Almost alien. Over time, through passes over each feature, more details were added. A few lines for the ears, followed by dots for the hairline, then light slashes as the crook of the eyebrows. The face then began to take on the slightest hint of emotion and personality. Before he got too far with the subject's head, Miles branched off with the neck, then a few strings of hair pulling away from the front and back of the skull. For a while he'd go back and forth—a few details to the face, then back to the neck, more hair filling in, a few areas of bone to add structure and shape to the body.

The process could be compared to lovemaking. Not a quickie where everything's rushed and frantic and desires are boiling, but more intimate and slow. Passionate. Attention placed all over, and never concentrated too long in one spot. The creation of this latest piece took on a binding, twisting of emotion and passion, with deep love and care paid through each stroke. Miles even found a few times in the midst of the project that his breathing had changed, had become shallow and rapid. His pulse picked up.

Never once did he tire sitting there. Not even one time did he feel the need or want to pause so he could stretch or take a break. His focus remained sharp. Every so often he'd gulp from the coffee cup that sat on the top mesh shelf of the desk, but he managed that without taking his eyes off the work. His appetite never returned after that can of tuna, not even a little. When late afternoon made the change over to evening and the croak and chirp and buzz of every night creature began, Miles hadn't noticed.

He just kept going. He added soft curves with the touchup of a kneaded eraser on an already pale line. When he finished with that he went the other way and put more weight and density into the waves of long hair. Slight smudges of his fingers gave blush to the face. The rim of the eraser on the Ticonderoga brushing the iris gave a contrast to the dark graphite and applied a shine in the eyes. Shadows formed by heavier touches of the pencil spread over areas of the subject like a dark water that brought out a definition of everything that made it so beautiful.

In all his years doing portraits on the side, Miles found difficulty having a live subject sitting posed behind his canvas. People had a hard time accepting their faults, a hard time seeing the truth—the minute creases, the worry lines, birthmarks, the slightest sag or evidence of age—even though he took great care in how his works would be viewed by others much harsher than himself, and he was his own worst critic. And being the harshest critic of his critics, even Miles was deeply touched by what he was doing; what was looking back at him from the surface of his latest work.

At just over three hours spent working, hovering over the canvas nitpicking every single detail, the final adjustments were made. With gentle brushes using the pad of his already silver index finger, he softened the ends of hair, the curve of the cheek, ran a path over the naked skin beneath the clavicle where it faded off into the white of the canvas.

Then, with a relieved sigh that felt like the first breath he'd taken since the beginning, it was done.

Straightening up on the stool brought a symphony of complaints from the muscles in his neck, tense all throughout, and a creaking of the rungs low on his spine. He massaged the overworked muscles of his right hand, cracking the swollen knuckles. All the while he stared at the finished picture with admiration and satisfaction, and exhaustion. And love.

All it needed was a title.

He scratched a single word—*Kindred*—on the back portion of the frame and then returned the canvas to the slanted table top, absorbing the whole of his work under the glow of the single bulb in the adjustable spotlight.

It was one thing to see her in the visions his memory would recall, to look at her in the photos around the house. It became something else to look at a beautiful rendition of Stephanie created by his own hand.

Quickly he was overwhelmed. A fresh and fierce stinging crawled into his eyes. A few tears welled up and held in place, blurring his sight. No longer was he the artist—even his most critical side remained silent for what he was taking in while looking at this new picture. What part solely remained of him sitting there was the widowed husband.

Many tears were shed and minutes were lost as he sat there, the scar of his loss aching.

The foyer was a combination of dim light—catching a residual orange shine coming in through the row of windows in the living room—and inky shadows. The streetlamps lining Edgebrook gave off a dull glow in the late night gloom. Miles set his empty mug next to the coffeemaker, a quarter of a fresh pot remained and was being kept hot, and then walked through the living room back out into the foyer. There was no sign of Ava.

He rubbed his weary, cried-out eyes, then made his way upstairs. Other than to once clean up and make the bed, he hadn't set foot in the master bedroom—the scene of his wife's murder, and ironically the last place he saw her alive—since that afternoon he left. Whether it was out of the pure exhaustion lumbering through his strung-out body and mind, or the bit of hope he chose to hold on to, or maybe even both that he didn't dwell much on being inside the room altogether.

He cracked open the windows to air out the stagnant smell. The right side of the king-size bed was hers, the left had been his, and that's where he climbed in after peeling off the heavier covers and pulling up the sheets. There was a momentary catch in his throat—a swell of yearning—as he lay down facing Stephanie's side of the bed. Miles reached out and laid a hand across to her side.

He was asleep when the curtains fluttered from the soft breeze sliding in. Off in the distance came the first rumbles of thunder over the hills.

The dream continued, as if a bookmark had been placed where it previously ended.

While sharing stories of doomed past relationships, the beautiful woman sitting across from him in the Italian restaurant told a story about a guy she had planned to meet but cancelled after a sudden, strange feeling came over her.

"I got this . . . this strange feeling." He watched her place her hand over her chest. "It was like pins and needles, like when your foot falls asleep and you try to move it. In an instant everything felt wrong, just very wrong."

He asked if she met the man despite her feeling.

"I couldn't get the thought out of my head that something terrible would happen if I did."

And she was right. He watched her drain her wine glass before explaining that not long after the date was cancelled she learned this man had gone on a rage—breaking into the apartment of his ex-girlfriend, murdering her and the man she was with.

"It could have been me, Miles," she said.

He didn't know what to say.

"That feeling . . ." she said, "the one I told you about. I think it was my guardian angel looking out for me."

Though he was skeptical, he kept that to himself.

The woman said, "That night, when I got that feeling, it was like . . . affirmation, you know? I could sense it somehow."

She lifted her water glass to meet his for a toast. "It's like you said: Even the strangest things happen for a reason."

Their glasses clinked, and when they did Miles opened his eyes.

The words lodged in the front of his mind.

Guardian angel.

The rain was still miles off to the west. The rumblings of thunder were so distant, and Miles so hazy in the realm between being awake and asleep, the sound could have been mistaken for a train of large trucks passing by on the nearby parkway. Otherwise the blanket of surrounding summer dark consisted of nothing more than the consistent chirp of crickets and the gentle brush of sweet-scented breeze slipping in through the open windows. There was no comprehension of time. There was nothing he knew in those first few seconds of wakefulness. Except warmth, and the dream.

In his waking mind, drifts of them at the table together in the Italian restaurant still continued to play.

He asked if she ever got the strange feeling about him, to which she turned her eyes up to him with intent, a string of pasta slurped up between her pursed lips.

"No," she said. "You're a good guy, Miles."

He made a joke about always being considered the good guy by every girl he knew all his life, flashing a grin.

The waking Miles had the same grin on his face.

She asked, "Am I like every girl?"

"No," he said. Miles, in his bed, said this same thing at the same time. "Not at all."

It was then he felt something around the inside of his right leg down around the shin. In the restaurant he almost jumped out of his seat until the realization came over him. It was her leg slipping around his. Under the table she had slipped off one of her boots. The soft, warm feel of her naked calf against him brought a deep blush to his face and neck. He was staring into her eyes. Nothing else mattered.

In the bed he once shared with his wife, Miles made to roll from his left side onto his back, grunting at a tightness in his lower spine from the hours spent on the stool hunched over the canvas. But just as he was about to make the turn, he stopped.

Something was wrapped over his left leg.

With a stifled gasp he came fully awake, his eyes wide open in the dark. Instantly the webs of synapses crossing through his brain fired, the rest of the dream lost but the connections made, and it registered that particular touch as Stephanie—how he had awakened days earlier to the same touch only to discover that, in the light, she wasn't there.

This time though it was different—he sensed something more than just her touch with him. And though his vision, blurry without his glasses on, made it difficult to determine much in the dark beside him, he knew Stephanie was there, in some form, on her side of the bed—the lower half of her leg entwined with his. His hand, the one he left lingering over on the far side of the bed after climbing in, was raised. There was a warmth, the form of something under the sheet. A shape. The countless times during their twelve years of marriage they'd fallen asleep and awakened like this cycled through his mind. An already racing heartbeat from the initial jolt of waking hammered harder as the pieces started coming together at the revelation of the picture. Where before he had been afraid of moving out of fear of losing the feeling of her, Miles realized he was responsible for what was happening.

He had made the picture of her.

You've been given an exceptional gift, Miles.

He could hear Ava's voice in his head, speaking softly over the drumming of his heart, like she were right there with him. He supposed, in a way, she *had* always been there with him.

You can use it to choose how to remember your wife. And say goodbye.

He let those words tumble over and over in his head.

Say goodbye.

Say goodbye.

This was his moment.

This was his chance to heal.

With no telling just how long he had, Miles found all the words he ever dreamt of saying to his late wife flooding into the back of his throat. Over the last nine months it seemed he'd daydreamt a million times over what he would say to Stephanie if he'd ever gotten the chance to talk to her just one more time. Visiting her plot at Hillside Cemetery wasn't the same. Yes, he was talking to her, but she wasn't there. Her body, an empty vessel, was underground. Her stone was there. Her flowers were there. But she was gone.

Now, through one exceptional gift, he had found her.

And he also found that when he stopped worrying about what to say and just focused on the thought of her being there, sleeping soundly beside him, the words found their own way out, shaky through his trembling lips, at the volume of a whisper.

"I'm sorry I left you."

Along with his words, tears also found their way out, seeping into his pillow.

"I had a bad feeling," he said. "I knew I shouldn't have left. I felt it. It still haunts me."

He drew in a long breath and cleared his throat against the emotions threatening to reduce him to sobs that would steal his voice.

"You once told me about a bad feeling you had . . . and how it saved your life. I should have known. I should have listened to myself. I let you down, babe. I let us both down."

The pooling of tears soaking into the pillowcase were cool against his cheek. His focus remained on the moment, on the touch of her skin against his, trusting that the things he'd walled up for so long, all the guilt he held on to, would continue to pour out before this moment with her would be over.

"You wanted to be a mother so badly, and I failed us."

It had been this horrible burden carried over the years that panged inside of him like a throbbing migraine, always beneath the surface even when it was dormant. It flared up whenever he thought of a child of their own—a child he could never give her, and one he so desperately wanted. But this was the time and the opportunity to finally put it behind him.

"But you were right, you know . . . There is such a thing as guardian angels. I think I met mine. Her name is Ava. I think she's here because of you. And I just want you to know . . . She saved me."

The tears stopped falling. The muscles in his throat relaxed. Miles thought he felt a slight flex of her leg around his shin, as if to affirm everything he had come to believe about the mysterious woman who appeared in the apartment above him, who had awakened a unique power hiding inside of him, however temporary or long lasting it would prove to be. Miles gave a gentle squeeze to his wife. Following a long exhale he felt a sigh in his heart as the sorrow long carried on his back and inside his chest had been exhausted. A cresting in the wave of his grief. The next breath he took in felt new, and full of hope.

"I love you," he said. "I love you so much."

For as long as he was able, Miles remained still. His heart found a slower rhythm. Before too long the cadence of his breathing began lulling him back to sleep. He couldn't fight it for long.

"Goodnight sweetie."

She would be gone the next time he woke. He knew it even then. There also wouldn't be any more visions invading his dreams, or, he suspected, not even the phantom feeling of her when he woke. He'd said what he needed to, said his goodbyes, and now Miles Greene could find comfort in a more peaceful rest.

So he took this last moment—this last lingering of her touch—all the way into the depths of his sleep.

Sometime later, still in the dead of night, a crackle of thunder reached in and pulled him out of that sleep. A flash of light beyond his closed eyes nudged him further awake. At first Miles resisted, but the resounding thunderclap made it impossible to ignore. For a moment he lay there, listening to the first drops of rain as they sprinkled on the roof and the skylight above his head. Still in the soupy mix between being awake and dozing, he rolled onto his back and was quick to notice that he was indeed alone in the bed. Reaching over to the vacant side, his hand lay flat against the cool mattress.

He was content to remain just this way and listen as the middle of the night rainfall rolled on by. Until an explosion of glass nearly brought him out of his skin.

His muscles and joints locked. A spell of haziness passed behind his eyes—the blood rushing away from his head and running to the farthest reaches of his limbs to the tips of his extremities—but faded quickly. He swallowed down his heart when it felt as if it would escape out through his mouth. Then he listened.

The noise had been downstairs. Foyer maybe. Living room maybe. He couldn't pinpoint the origin. No sound other than the steadying rain followed it. The echo of the explosion had carried off the marble floors so it could have been anywhere downstairs, whether that was the living room, the foyer, or the kitchen. The sound itself was undeniable though. Something had been broken.

Lightning sizzled and flashed through the skylight. Thunder exploded above. The rustling of the trees picked up.

And now his bladder was begging to be emptied.

A peek out into the open hall overlooking the foyer gave him nothing. A brilliant flickering of lightning strikes illuminated much of the first floor. Nothing looked different. The storm was almost directly overhead—the immediate follow-up growl of thunder shook the foundation as he took the stairs down.

He was about ten steps from the kitchen, in the middle of the foyer, when the bottom of his right foot went down over something small, cold, and sharp.

His immediate reaction at the piercing of his heel was to pick up his foot as if he'd just stepped on a hot coal, maintaining balance with small hops on the opposite foot until he got a hand on the closest wall. Quickly he found and plucked a small piece of glass from his heel, at the same time a gust of cold wind came from the direction of the front door.

The sound of driving rain and the wild elements was much clearer. Because no longer was there a window beside the front door to dampen the sound.

A strike of blue light lit up the foyer, revealing not only the naked slot that had once been a window—the same tall, slender piece of glass beside the door that had been broken the night of his wife's murder—but also the trail of shards and pebbles coming inside. Spread out all around him the sparkling pieces of glass lit up, reflecting the flashing blue.

A few shards were still lodged in the frame, hanging like wayward teeth. A few loose pieces dangled, some shook loose in the wind and blew across the floor towards him. The image of this struck Miles with the numbing terror of being all too familiar.

There was nothing around him that was visible in the foyer to suggest any debris of the storm had been responsible for the broken window. No small branch or tree limb or stone used as a torpedo by the wind, nothing to disavow what his fears were now suggesting.

A small throbbing began around his temples, making his head spin.

He had seen this before. And not just the night of his wife's death.

In the drawing.

"My God . . ." he gasped aloud, and despite the sharp ache in the bleeding wound on his foot, Miles was already running.

A cordless phone hung just inside the kitchen next to the light switch. The fact that he continued paying the phone bill was now nothing short of a miracle.

Drops of heavy rain chased him across the marble floor as it was swept inside by the wind. Miles managed to flip on the light in the kitchen and grab the phone affixed to the wall, his thumb froze after pressing the nine button. That's as far as he got.

"Put it down."

The voice was tinged with desperation, but forcibly stern. It came out of the dark from the way of the dining room. Miles startled and looked to his left but saw no one in that entryway or the pass-thru. Not until the next flash of lightning revealed the silhouette.

"I said . . ." And there was a noticeable pause, before the figure owning the voice materialized out of the dark. ". . . put it down."

The voice wasn't familiar but the face was.

A frail and pale looking waif of a man standing about the same height as Miles, wearing a pair of dirty black jeans with blown out knees and a frayed brown tee that had a tear in the breast pocket, entered into the little bit of light shining in the kitchen. His wet skin glistened almost transparent. He stood paused in the entryway, right in front of the closed utility closet. His bony face, long withered away by obvious long years of drug use, was pockmarked and riddled with stubble. But it was the defining feature that sent a searing hot flash through Miles's brain: laced over the man's left eye was a scar; a scar that began its trail just above the eyebrow and carved a winding path down along the inside of the nose and turned out into the middle of the cheek, like a backwards C, before ending just below the rigid jaw.

This ghastly face had been the same one sketched out in pencil by Miles's own hand just days earlier. The sheet of sketch paper that featured the disturbing work had been discarded to the floor in his apartment, but here the man stood in real life, in the flesh.

The Scarred Man.

The picture had come to life.

And while his mere presence was threatening enough, the ragged intruder was clutching a large kitchen knife in one trembling, vein-covered hand. There was a single piece of cutlery missing from the wooden block on the counter space near the pass-thru.

The Scarred Man, dark circles surrounding sunken, wily eyes that didn't blink, seemed unable to control his withdrawal-induced tremors. The knife's serrated edge and tip pointed right at Miles, quivering, the grip on the handle tight but shaky.

Miles waited, heart beating madly, frozen in place, for the intruder to say something else, or make a move of some kind.

The Scarred Man swallowed deep, the blue wiry cords in his neck standing out. He made a gesture at the phone with his knife. "I'm not gonna tell you again."

Miles held up his empty hand in a pleading gesture that said he'd do whatever he was asked while he returned the cordless phone back onto the receiver. Unlike the strung-out man holding him at knifepoint, Miles was steady. But this was deceiving. Just beneath the visible surface he was absolutely terrified.

"Now," said The Scarred Man, his knife dancing with his words, "you and I are gonna go up, and you're gonna open the safe."

As soon as this registered with Miles, a crack of thunder split the heavens.

"What?" whispered Miles, then, louder, "What did you say?"

The Scarred Man's wretched pale face lifted with a wry half-grin. His dark, vile eyes twinkled. "The safe, I said." He spoke slowly, clearly. "*You are . . . going to open . . . the safe.*"

A momentary daze akin to déjà vu breezed over Miles. He felt woozy, short of breath, and very warm. Before he could recover a succession of rapid-fire flashes blitzed his mind.

First he saw *The Storm*. His sketch of dark, violent skies battering the ascending Edgebrook Road. In the vision he had cut a run through the downpour to stand just far enough from his house to see a light on inside.

A light that could have been coming from the kitchen.

Just as it was happening now.

Then he got a vision of his sketch of the broken window. It had been the first thing he had seen and remembered from the night he arrived home to learn of his wife's murder. The sight of evidence markers placed among the widespread piles of shards and pebbles of glass as two officers snapped pictures was what confirmed for him, before anyone had said it, that his wife was dead.

The same window that had been broken again. And only one person he knew of could have slipped through that narrow opening.

Miles didn't even realize his fists were clenching. All he could feel was a drumming in his temples, the rising heat of blood burning his face. A blinding hatred overcame him that, if it were a flame, could scorch a forest and reduce it to ash. "It was you," he said, and then he swallowed. "*You* killed my wife."

His accusation was met with a long silence as the rain continued to fall.

And it was in that silence that the confirmation revealed itself, in those twinkling dark eyes, in the absolute lack of surprise in the ruined face of The Scarred Man, who didn't so much as flinch at being called a murderer.

It was the knife that eventually responded, rising a few inches; the grip around the handle tightening and, now, the blade didn't shake at all. "No one was supposed to be home." His head cocked to the side then and started shaking back and forth. He was trying to justify what he had done, absolving his part in it by deflecting blame. "No one was supposed to get hurt."

All this did was further incite Miles.

"She had called the police." The Scarred Man swallowed and licked at his dry, cracked lips. The knife still aimed at Miles. "She saw my face."

Another picture came in a flash. This one of the steaming mug he'd drawn before leaving the apartment to come home. On that wintry

February afternoon over twelve years ago he had been holding that hot mug as he sat in the lounge area of the Sunset Moon Café, where he first met Stephanie. He'd been keeping his hands warm, attempting to settle his nerves, watching out the storefront window for her to pass by in the blustery day.

And now he noticed, on the countertop just an arm's length away, in the space between himself and The Scarred Man, was his mug from earlier that evening; it was empty sitting beside the coffeemaker. The burner of the coffeemaker was still on; the glass pot still a quarter full.

This can't be coincidence, he thought. *It can't be.*

The Scarred Man . . . The Storm . . . The Broken Window . . . The Coffee Mug . . .

Even the painting of Ava and the picture of Stephanie.

He had been wrong this whole time. His pictures hadn't been coming to life at all.

They had been showing him his future.

They had been preparing him for this exact moment.

"All I want," said The Scarred Man, flicking his tongue over his sore lips again, and moving the knife once again with his demands, "is money." He twitched. "I know you have it. I know you're some famous artist. That's all I want. You don't have to end up like your old lady."

But Miles wasn't even listening. It had dawned on him in his revelation that there was a missing picture in the sequence. *The Painted Lady.* The sketch of the butterfly. The first picture he had been inspired to draw while sitting in his truck at the stoplight, knowing that he'd have to come up with something for his art exhibition at the Garland. Seeing the butterfly coast over the outside of his windshield brought on the first flash that sent him back to an overcast day long ago when he and Stephanie had released a similar, newly-hatched creature out into the world.

It was his only picture that hadn't been realized that evening. But Miles didn't have to wonder about it for much longer.

The Painted Lady made its appearance at the same time something else took place. Something that could have been interpreted as a complete coincidence, or rather something extraordinary that fate had written among the stars.

Remaining on the dining room side of the entryway, The Scarred Man was standing a few feet in front of the door to the small utility closet that was just off of the kitchen. What he didn't know because he couldn't see it, was that the door behind him was now slowly, and silently, opening.

It was after moving into the house that Miles and his wife noticed the utility door never stayed shut on its own so he installed a secondary turn lock above the handle. That door had been standing open earlier when he came home, and he had closed it. But for some unknown reason he had neglected to set the turn lock to keep it from opening. And it just so happened to be opening now, revealing the empty inside of the closet.

Empty except for the Painted Lady that appeared.

Perhaps it had been inside the house all along and Miles hadn't seen it; perhaps it had gotten trapped in the utility closet when he closed the door. Perhaps this was all coincidence.

Or, perhaps, much like the door opening on its own at this very moment, like the sudden appearance of a man with a scar tracing down his face—the very same man who happened to be the one who murdered his wife nine months ago and gotten away, the butterfly, the last event Miles foreshadowed with his drawings, was, like Ava, a little bit of divine intervention.

Regardless, as soon as the little winged creature came out of the dark behind The Scarred Man, Miles knew what he had to do, and he had to do it fast.

The butterfly made a beeline and skimmed over the stubbly head of The Scarred Man, swooping back low over his face. His jumpy reaction—the flinch of the hand that held the knife, his dark eyes off Miles momentarily as he aimed to swat away the insect—was enough of a distraction.

Miles went for the handle of the coffee mug. It was in his hand less than a second before he threw it at the Scarred Man, who dodged the mug but was unable to avoid the swinging coffeepot that came after. In a swift, committed, fluid motion Miles took two leaping steps and reared back, following up with all of his might. The Scarred Man's dark eyes flicked over in the direction of the incoming glass pot much too late. His gaunt face distorted upon impact. The pot erupted in a splash of broken glass and hot coffee. Only the brown plastic handle remained whole in Miles's grip. Splotches of hot coffee singed his hand, but the rushing adrenaline prevented him any pain.

The Scarred Man, however, howled in agony.

Miles didn't waste a second. With everything he could muster, and there was a lot considering his rage, he forced the scalded and stunned murderer into the open closet behind the entryway and slammed the door shut. Miles put his weight against the door and threw the turn lock.

The cries of pain from within did nothing to dispel Miles's anger. They only infuriated him more. So, without a second thought, he released the lock, opened the door and grabbed the sobbing intruder by the neck before throwing three good punches to the head. The screams ceased immediately. The Scarred Man slumped down to the closet floor, unconscious.

Miles slammed the door shut again and turned the lock. Breathing heavy, he put his hands on his knees—the right one throbbing. When he grabbed the cordless phone to dial 911 he had to do everything with his left hand. The right one was swelling and singing in all octaves of pain when the adrenaline began wearing off. It was likely broken. But it was worth it. Even if he could never draw again it was worth it.

And it wasn't the pain in his right hand that brought tears to his eyes. After speaking to the emergency dispatcher, Miles began sobbing uncontrollably.

They were tears of relief.

Of rejoice.

The storm diminished shortly after the call was made to 911. Everything quickly began to dry out from the prevailing southerly winds ushering in. Miles sat out on the stone front steps of his house, looking every so often far off in the distance toward the eastern hills where a few flickers of lightning lit up the retreating storm clouds. Overhead was a clear and brilliant starry night.

Swirling emergency lights shined in his eyes every few seconds. The lights also bounced off parked vehicles and surrounding homes. Concerned neighbors craned their necks out their front doors and from behind closed window drapes and shades, trying for a better look at the all-too-similar scene playing out on the block. They gathered in the early morning hour around the sawhorses set up by police, creating a perimeter around the six police response units and the one ambulance called to the scene.

Two officers walked past Miles and into the house, their jobs to fully document the scene. Miles paid them no mind. He kept his head bowed, cradling his sore and swollen right hand, coming to terms with it all. No one would believe it—especially not these cops who would be looking to fill out a report, eventually. So what would he tell them when it came time to give a statement?

While he contemplated this, a pair of shiny black shoes stopped in his presence on the front walk. The large frame of the man standing before him blocked out the swirling lights.

"Not the kind of thing you see too often."

Miles gave a shake of his head to Officer Voss—Cleveland as he had known him all these years. Cleveland hadn't been home across the street when the call came in. He'd been out on patrol. Miles said to him, "I wouldn't think so."

Cleveland cleared his throat. "Home owner who hasn't been occupying his own property in almost a year just happens to be home the exact night of a break-in? Add to that the person breaking in just so happens to be the one responsible for the murder of that man's wife?" Cleveland shook his head. "Like I said: not the kind of thing you see too often."

Miles understood Cleveland's reluctance to chalk it all up to coincidence, but the truth was stranger than his tale that reeked of fiction. He kept his story to Cleveland at just the facts, reiterating his original call to 911 where he calmly stated that he had an intruder subdued in a closet and was in need of help. To add or suggest anything else—anything supernatural—that might have influenced the turn of events was not the kind of thing that could be documented in a police report. It would make them both look crazy. And Miles had just gotten over believing that he was.

"I think he just kept waiting for me to come back," Miles said. "He couldn't have gotten into the safe without me opening it or giving him the combination." A pause. "Has he said anything?"

A smile crossed the officer's moustached face. "You'd think the burns he suffered would've been enough to silence him for a while."

"So he did say something?"

"You may not believe it any more than I do," Cleveland said with a shake of his head, and this coming from a man who'd served on the force in one manner or another over seventeen years. He'd probably seen things beyond belief more than once.

"I'm open to anything," Miles said.

Cleveland took a seat next to him on the stair. The flashing lights now in both of their faces as they looked out into the front yard at the officers wrapping things up. "He told us he got . . . a feeling. Didn't know how to explain it other than to say this feeling told him you'd be here tonight." He paused. "Now ain't *that* sounding like some crazy batshit?"

Miles let this sink in. He then lied. "You're right; I don't believe it. But I guess his feeling was right."

The two officers that had gone inside to document came back out with their notepads and camera. Cleveland waited until they were out of earshot.

"He admitted to it all." A long, sincere pause where Cleveland turned and looked Miles in the face. The big man's eyes wavered. The shining lights revealed tears on the verge. "The van you said you saw that day? Well he claimed to have parked it in the woods somewhere down in Bucks County in PA and burned it the night of the murder. Our guys are checking up on that. But tonight he drove here in a dark blue Honda Civic and that was reported stolen.

"He'll be formally charged in the morning down at the courthouse. You don't have to be there, but . . . just in case."

Miles said he would be.

Officer Voss then put a hand on Miles's shoulder and squeezed before he stood. "Glad we finally got him."

Miles agreed.

"You might wanna get that hand looked at before the ambulance leaves. By the look of his eye you got a hell of a right hook. And you swing a pretty mighty coffeepot." Cleveland then flashed a wink with a smile and strode off to help start clearing out the other personnel. There was nothing more to be done that night.

Miles remained on the stair even as the first signs of daybreak crawled into town, and the last police cruiser pulled away from the house. When he felt ready again, he went inside.

Later that morning he spent a long time on the stoop outside of Ava's apartment, his right hand in an air-cast. He knew he could go inside if he wanted to but there was nothing behind the door for him except for an empty living space. He could knock on the door but she wouldn't answer.

He kept thinking that where he stood was where he had been the other night before his life changed. How much had happened since.

And now he missed her. He also wondered then if what she said in the truck would ever ring true. Would he eventually not think of her at all?

When he ventured back down to his apartment to begin gathering his things to pack, he was greeted by the sight of the Painted Lady. It flew a path around him and then landed on the nearby sill. The butterfly flexed its wings, as if signaling to him.

It would be a long time before he stopped thinking of Ava.

The diner at the Red Oak Inn was surprisingly sparse for a Friday evening. A family of four occupied the corner booth at the far right side of the eatery and an elderly couple talked over coffee and a shared piece of cheesecake in a booth under a bright bulb that cast long shadows over their faces that did their age no favors. A husky middle aged truck driver, sitting on a red leather stool up at the counter, hovered over his Danish while perusing the measly Sports section of the local Serling Oaks Times. Miles supposed business would pick up into the overnight hours, when college kids would need to sponge up all the booze they'd consumed with a thick stack of pancakes before heading back home or to their dorms.

A dark haired, raccoon-eyed waitress saddled up to the table.

"Ready to order, guys?"

Miles put in for a Caesar salad.

"Salad?" Bryan said, as in *are ya kiddin' me?*

"I'm a little nervous about tonight," said Miles. "May be hard for you to believe given the extra tire I've been carrying around lately, but I could never eat before an event. Besides, I've started being careful with what I'm eating and have been taking longer walks. I'm down seven pounds."

Bryan said, "Congrats, man, you look good."

"I feel good."

For himself Bryan ordered the Red Oak's signature Clogger, a two all-beef patty burger with lettuce, tomatoes, smoked honey BBQ sauce, with thinly sliced fried onions, and a spicy mayo between toasted seeded buns. His own diet pushed to the side for tonight. "When I get nervous, I eat."

Once their waitress left for the kitchen to put in their order, Bryan mentioned stopping by The Garland Gallery that morning. "Love all the new stuff," he said. "But it's all sketches. Only one painting?"

That one painting was the only one Miles had done in the last eight months. No one else had ever seen it because it spent most of its time in a black plastic bag in the back corner of the basement at the apartment.

"Don't get me wrong," Bryan said, "the painting's gorgeous, and the woman's hot, but it just doesn't fit the theme of what you've got going on." He then paused. "Is there a theme?"

Miles shrugged. "It's all I have. For now."

To him the painting and six other sketches (the ones done on sketch paper were professionally framed while the canvas art was left to hang bare on the Garland's interior brick walls) did carry a theme. A personal one. With specific instructions that the works be hung in a certain order (the order they were created with his first *Painted Lady* and ending with *Kindred*, the drawing of his wife), the sequence of pictures told the story that had brought him out of his rut, and had healed him.

The onlookers at the Garland that night would never realize the link running through his works and that was okay. The pictures weren't for the onlookers. They were for himself.

"So, Miles." Bryan gave a shift of an eyebrow in the moment's hesitation. "Anything ever happen with the woman who lived above when you were at the apartment? Tell me all the disgusting details."

Much as he had with the police investigating the break-in at the house, Miles found it easier to go with fiction rather than the truth.

"Well, sorry to disappoint you from hearing all the 'disgusting details,' but turns out she just kind of up and left one night."

Bryan was obviously disappointed to hear this. "So nothing?"

"The morning I left, I went up to let her know the downstairs was gonna be empty and her door was open. Nothing inside. She was gone."

"That's too bad. Hope she wasn't skipping out on rent."

The waitress returned to refill Bryan's coffee. Miles tossed him a creamer.

"Landlord sad to see you go?"

Miles shrugged. "She understood."

And she did. While Ms. Hutchings would have loved to have kept Miles forever—good tenant, paid early, never complained or caused trouble—she wished him well. Perhaps to keep from revealing how much it personally affected her, the old, raspy-toned landlady abruptly ended their phone conversation by saying his security deposit would be in the mail.

It arrived at the house three days later.

"So you're all settled back in?"

"Still settling," Miles said. "But glad to be home." He wasn't yet about to mention to his brother-in-law agent that he was going to be taking on a few jobs soon. There were a few clients out west that he'd spoken to directly and were excited to learn he was working his way back into the biz. But Miles didn't want this turning into a business dinner. This was a celebratory meal.

Less than ten minutes later their Clogger and salad arrived.

Three-quarters through his burger—and amazingly yet to drop even a single bit of the honey BBQ on his nice shirt—Bryan answered a phone call.

"Someone more important than me?" Miles asked.

Bryan told whoever was on the other end that they were inside at a booth on the left. He then hung up and regarded Miles. "Not just someone."

"But still more important than me?"

Moments later Bryan looked up at the jingling of the diner's front door being opened. Miles turned to look over his shoulder. In walked an elderly couple Miles knew immediately despite not having seen for a while; the stout man wore a full white beard and a tan blazer with pants of a navy blue shade, and was arm-in-arm with a woman of similar stature in a white wind jacket over an orange and pink striped sundress, sporting a frizzy do. Both walked slowly, each with their own obvious aches and pains working against their better efforts.

Bryan stood to greet them. "Ma, Dad, glad you guys made it."

Miles knew them as Hank and Marion.

"Well, we would've been here sooner," said Marion, "but your father did forty-five all through Massachusetts."

"It was a construction zone," Hank argued. "And it wasn't the *entire* state." The rugged old man then set his sights on Miles and reached out with a large, arthritis-stricken hand. "Heya Miles, how's it goin'?"

Miles stood and shook with his father-in-law. "Uh, good, good. I didn't know you were coming down."

"Yeah, well, we heard some big shot artist had himself a show or something. Thought we'd check it out." Hank then tossed a wink and smile.

Miles greeted Marion with a kiss on the cheek. The four barely all fit in the booth. The raccoon-eyed waitress was quick to return and offer coffee and a dessert menu.

"Nah, no thanks," said Hank. "I ate already."

"Hank," snapped Marion, "that was two hours ago when we stopped for gas and you had a Snickers bar."

"It was King-sized!"

Marion ordered a coffee.

"How long are you guys in town?" asked Miles.

"Heading back up tomorrow," Marion said. "Hank's got some lawn duties to get done."

Hank sighed. "Well, if you hadn't gotten rid of Thomas he could've come over yesterday and had it all done."

Marion waved this off. "Thomas is too expensive."

"He's twelve!" Hank said. "He'd be happy if you paid him with a happy meal."

Miles and Bryan shared a look that said things never change. Bryan then announced they should get going. "Probably wouldn't look good if the featured artist wasn't there when the gallery opened their doors to their own exhibit."

The clock on the dashboard read ten minutes to seven. Ten minutes before the First Friday Art Walk would officially begin in downtown Serling Oaks. Ten minutes before Miles would complete making a comeback to his old ways of life.

He fired up the engine of his pickup and coasted to a stop at the parking lot's exit. He waited for Hank and Marion to come up behind him in their Lincoln Continental so they could follow. Before he took his foot off the brake, he considered what was to come of the evening, and beyond.

All there was left for him to do was apply the gas, head for the highway, and follow the ribbon of roadways toward the lit-up string of galleries downtown.

Miles did just that.

There were some familiar faces among the crowd along with many Miles did not recognize. According to Liza, curator of the Garland, and sharply-dressed in her turquoise blazer and black skirt, attendance for the event had reached capacity for the small museum. During her lengthy introduction for the evening she apologized for having to turn people away.

"This never happens!" Her face was lit up with astonishment as she went on saying that this was a good problem for them to have. "We always offer free wine during our art walk events and not even *that* coaxes people to show up."

The standing crowd of one-twenty-five laughed in unison. Some held up their plastic wine cups and offered suggestions for better wines to keep them coming back in the future. This, also, was met with bursts of laughter all around the room.

"So thank you," said Liza. "Thank you for coming out and showing up tonight to support us and to support a wonderfully talented, home-grown artist. Many of you have probably seen his work and not even realized it." She then went on to list numerous examples of feature films he had created the poster art for, along with a few mentions of book titles where he had done the illustrations—all listed for her to read off on the back of a white index card that he filled out in a nervous scribble right before the evening started with a right hand that was still healing.

"I'll have him say a few words and then, please, stick around, mingle, check out his beautiful work, drink our wine!"

More laughs.

"Let's welcome our featured artist for the month of July, born and raised here in Serling Oaks, Mister Miles Greene."

Standing just five feet off to Liza's left, right next to Bryan and Molly (who was holding a sleeping Lily), Miles stepped forward to warm applause. He joined Liza in front of the brick wall in the back of the museum where his pictures hung under warm spotlights.

Liza left him alone in front of the crowd as the reception dwindled to quiet. The room suddenly grew warmer despite the loud air conditioning. Miles could feel sweat underneath his corduroy blazer. The pause waiting for him to speak went on for a while as he searched the crowd, spotting faces he knew. Bryan, Molly, and sleeping Lily, of course. His in-laws. Towards the middle of the room was Doctor Havish Andrews and his wife, Bhavna. Cleveland was standing in the back, tossing up a thumb in the air in a show of support, his large frame impossible to miss.

This was one of those times when, looking around, Miles wished he could've seen his own parents standing together in the room, sharing in the celebration of an accomplishment of his. Given that they weren't around anymore he liked to think they were there with him in others ways, and still watching. Like Stephanie.

"I should probably tell you now that I am not the greatest speaker." He shrugged, his head tipped downward. "That's why I decided to be an artist instead of something like . . . President of the United States."

The crowd laughed. He could feel their support.

He tried his best to look around the room. "Many of you know more about my personal life than my professional one. I'm sure you've seen things on the news or in the paper the last couple of months. Back when everything happened . . . this was the last place I ever thought I would be again—standing in front of people, talking about my drawings. I actually never thought I would work again. I have my agent and brother to thank for this."

Bryan smiled.

"He'll be the first to tell you he got me to do this after a whole lot of kicking and screaming."

Bryan nodded. There were a few more scattered laughs throughout the crowd.

"Certainly it's been an unusual path and a strange ride getting here."

Miles thought of the pictures mounted on the wall behind him. They began with the painting (the only painting chosen for the display) of Ava, which, for the purposes of the show, he titled as *The Painted Lady #2*.

"I won't even try to lie to you—the artwork on display here tonight isn't my best; I've done better, and bolder. Some of my wife's favorite pieces of mine were the ones I did for no other reason than I wanted to." He was speaking of The Quiet Ones. "Those were the pieces not for sale. They really weren't meant for eyes other than my own and those closest.

"But, in getting to this point I realized that there is a plan. It took me a while but I eventually saw it. A lot of wonderful people here tonight . . . and some that aren't . . . helped me to see it. This show wouldn't be if not for them."

He took a breath as a small, modest applause broke out. Miles made sure to connect with each of the faces he knew—those that he wanted to know he was appreciative of.

"I think the pictures on the wall behind me are the perfect representations of me. They weren't purchased or commissioned. I didn't follow anyone else's instructions or abide by their wants. These are mine, each of them. They are me. And they tell a story." He paused. "And if that story had a theme . . . it would be something I once told the woman who became my wife."

He paused again.

"Even the strangest things happen for a reason."

Abruptly, he ended there.

Liza led a modest applause as Miles walked off the center of the floor. Within moments the room was back to mingling.

"Congratulations, Miles," said Molly, her hips gently swaying. Sleeping Lily drooling on her shoulder. "This is beautiful."

"Thank you, Molly." He then turned his attention to Bryan. "I'm gonna duck out I think."

Creases formed in Bryan's brow. "Already? It just started. You're the star here, homes. And after that kickass speech?"

Miles patted him on the shoulder. "Not really feeling like mingling. Plus I've got to make a stop on the way home. I trust you'll give them a good excuse for me."

Bryan winked. "Got you covered."

It was just after eight fifteen when he arrived at Hillside Cemetery. The groundskeeper, ID tag reading Chet, cleaning off his riding mower outside the main gate, told him he had ten minutes. Miles said he would be out in five.

He parked and got out holding a dozen white gerbera daisies.

Under a weeping willow that was swaying in the gentle night breeze on the hill at sunset, Miles knelt down and placed the flowers on the grave marked STEPHANIE JUDITH GREENE.

As always when he made a visit, Miles put a hand on the top ridge of the stone.

"Well hun," he said, "I did it."

The last part in the process of The Work is the most difficult for any artist.

After all of the effort and time put in, after all of the mistakes, corrections, and sacrifices, and after all of the second-thoughts, doubts, and triumphs, there comes a time when nothing more can be done. The picture must live on its own.

And the time comes where the artist must let go.

He had just finished putting some touchups to a canvas when the doorbell rang. The newest picture—an acrylic painting—detailed the lone silhouette of a gunslinger, standing on the white sand of a vast desert. In the clear sky above The Stranger were many different worlds, some climbing over the horizon, others setting, all fading like crescent moons into the hazy distance. The stars twinkled above him as much as the millions upon millions of grains of sand under his boots.

This was the first picture upon returning to work.

Miles set his brush down and reviewed the work-in-progress. He felt the studio that commissioned him for the piece would be satisfied. He felt pretty good about it.

The doorbell called for him again.

Miles gave a final once over and then headed out of the studio. This image nor any other he would later create would have a life beyond the surface it was made on; there were no more flashes or vivid dreams; no more phantom touches when we woke. Whatever ability he was once graced with was no longer with him.

The walls of the narrow hall leading to the steps up to the foyer were now lined with the pictures of Ava (*The Painted Lady #2*), *The Scarred Man*, *The Painted Lady*, *The Broken Window*, *The Mug*, and *Kindred*. Normally Miles didn't hang his own work in the house for display, but these ones he couldn't bring himself to put away or leave sitting on the floor of his studio. Especially the one of his wife.

He lingered too long—the doorbell rang once more.

"Coming!" he called while racing up the short steps to the foyer. Where such a small exertion such as that would, at one time, reduce him to labored huffing and puffing, lately he had been experimenting with a walking/jogging program app that he'd downloaded on his phone. The goal at the end of the program was to run a 5K but Miles wasn't even considering doing that. He was enjoying the exercise every morning, feeling his stamina strengthen, doing what he could when it came to the running intervals, and later seeing the results on the scale. Wherever he went there was an added bounce to his step. The added combination of watching his meals and no longer taking the Ambien helped him to drop twelve more pounds. He needed to go shopping to get some clothes in the next size down. Bad enough most of his pants were loose and hung just below the start of his ass crack.

Through the thin window next to the front door—now restored and done so with a bulletproof glass to keep it from shattering—he could see who was waiting out on the stoop, and opened the door.

Molly greeted him with her flashing smile. "Hey Miles."

Miles welcomed them all—giving Molly a hug, Bryan a handshake, and a smiling baby Lily a gentle touch on her cheek.

"So, you ready for this?" Bryan said.

Miles grinned at Lily. "You bet. Been looking forward to it all week."

Molly handed over a pink-and-gray-checkered canvas bag full of books, toys, food, and plenty of spare diapers and wipes. "She'll be ready to eat in another hour, then she'll want to play. At about three o'clock she'll get cranky and will probably be ready for a nap."

Miles nodded. "Got it." He'd spent the last week converting the guest bedroom upstairs into a space more suitable for his young nieces to visit and stay over if their parents were ever in need of a reprieve.

"We wrote it all down for you," Bryan said, handing over a folded list from his back pocket.

"You'll be great," added Molly.

Bryan handed over Lily. "Lucky for you she pooped just before we left the house, so she's changed."

Molly jutted a thumb in her husband's direction. "He wanted to save it for you."

"Guy's gonna have to do it sometime," Bryan said in his own defense. "By the way, homes, with girls it's always front to back with the wipes. Just file that bit of info away."

Miles laughed. "I'll try to remember. And I do appreciate that we're starting out with a fresh diaper."

"We'll be back in a couple hours with your big sis," Bryan said to Lily, then kissed her in the center of her forehead. Lily responded with a coo.

"We'll bring pizza for dinner," Molly said, then kissed her child bye. "If you need anything just call." She thanked Miles, who said he was happy to do it to get a chance to spend time with his niece after missing so much of her first year of life. He refused being paid and said to put it toward the pizza.

"You remember what to do if she cries, right?" asked Bryan.

Miles nodded. "I'll figure it out."

Molly pulled Bryan along.

Miles and Lily waited out on the stoop, him waving and then helping the child to wave as her parents drove off to pick up Myra, their eldest, from cheerleader camp. Not once while watching her mother and father leave did Lily moan or get upset. Miles saw this as a good sign.

When they were alone, he turned to Lily in his arms. "So, kiddo, you ready for this?"

She answered by grabbing hold of his beard. She cooed again.

"Yeah," he said, and smiled. "Me too."

Circumstances being what they were, Miles would never get to be a father; that was an unfortunate reality that no drawing and no miraculous set of circumstances would ever fix. But he would always be an uncle, and that had its advantages. Despite what cards were dealt to him, Miles felt that what he wound up with in the end amounted to a life good enough.

He stepped inside with Lily in one arm and her bag of tricks in the other.

A life good enough.

My goal with this book was to be different—a good different. Hope I didn't let any of you down. Thank you for letting me into your busy lives. Shall we do this again? Keep an eye out for *An Unexpected Visit* next year.

ACKNOWLEDGMENTS

My always amazing wife, Rebecca, puts up with my overall nuttiness, my hectic writing and editing schedule, as well as me changing my mind all the time in regards to when I'll finally let her read a draft. Bless her patience. I adore her. This book is a two hundred-plus page love letter to her.

Jessica Kristie at Winter Goose gave me endless support through the journey of this book and the creation of its cover design. She is awesome. Her continued faith in me is a constant reminder that I can reach greater distances as I continue to grow as an author.

My wonderful editor, James Logan Koukis, caught me where I stumbled (Thank you, James). Any little chips in the armor should be blamed on me for not listening. I don't always listen. Ask my wife.

Thanks also go out to my close circle (John C., John M., Adara, Bonnie, and Dave), who read early drafts and gave their opinions. Even when those early drafts get too wordy, they still can't wait to read the finished product. Bless 'em.

A note to those who introduce me to others as a "famous author": We both know the truth, but I appreciate the kindness. Thank you.

Finally, a few words for my daughter.

Through all the struggles, the uncertainty, the bouts of self-abuse to my confidence, and the moments of craziness where I wonder what I get myself into when writing a book, I need only to look at you to realize I can relax—I've already made something that's perfect.

ABOUT THE AUTHOR

As an author of adult and young-adult fiction, Joseph Falank has had many of his stories featured in magazines and online publications. He has written and directed over twenty independent films and is a performing member and manager of The Puzzled Players Comedy Improv Theater. Since 2002 he has worked with children, young adults, and special needs kids in a classroom setting from pre-K through grade twelve. Joseph lives with his family in his hometown of Binghamton, New York.

www.ingramcontent.com/pod-product-compliance
Lightning Source LLC
Chambersburg PA
CBHW051248250626
47155CB00009B/3209